CHOP,

The man executed a perfect straight arm karate thrust toward Remo's exposed neck.

Perfect, except Remo drove his own fingers like a wedge between the Oriental's fingers and through his radius and ulna, cracking the man's arm like a piece of kindling.

The shattering concussion exploded the Oriental back through the office window out onto the stone below, which he hit with a *thump*. Remo turned just as the second man fell on his own upraised fingernail. His torso sank to the floor and began to leak blood onto the carpet.

It was only then that Remo noticed the length and sharpness of the Oriental's fingernails, and then he noticed a paper-thin cut across the top of his right hand. Remo clenched his fist and watched a thin red line grow between his second and third finger. A tiny bead of blood crossed his wrist and disappeared into his shirt.

It had been so long since he had seen his own blood...

The Destroyer #29:

THE FINAL DEATH

Warren Murphy and Richard Sapir

DESTROYER BOOKS
WARREN MURPHY MEDIA LLC

THE DESTROYER #29: THE FINAL DEATH

This edition published in 2018 by Destroyer Books/Warren Murphy Media LLC.

ISBN-13: 978-1-944073-49-7

ISBN-10: 1-944073-49-3

Requests for reproduction or interviews should be directed to DestroyerBooks@gmail.com.

Front cover art by Gere Tactical

For Bob Waldron —
You are missed.

CHAPTER ONE

THE LAST PIECE OF MEAT Vinnie Angus ever ate was cut from the shoulder section of a steer that had been taken from the fields of a rancher near Wyoming and driven in a tractor-trailer slat truck to a train that took him and thousands just like him to an auction. The steer was stuck in a Midwestern bin, then paraded before fat cowboys wearing Stetson hats, Gant shirts, and Izod three-button V-neck sweaters with little green alligators over the left breast, cowboys who had not seen hard work in 20 years, give or take a year.

The steer was bought, with 300 others, by Texas Solly Weinstein who put him into another truck for the drive to the slaughterhouse.

Cold, bored men in flannel shirts and heavy corduroy pants prodded him out in the early Houston morning with electric-shock sticks, moving him first into the ear-marking bin, then the milk-wash canal, then into the feeding yard where he was fattened up to 1,200 pounds, give or take a pound.

Texas Solly, who spoke Hebrew with a twang every Saturday at the synagogue, had cooed and primped as Vinnie Angus' steer, now all fattened up, had been herded into another truck, telling him how good he looked and how big he was and what nice skin and good legs he had.

As the truck had moved off, Texas Solly had gone inside and sold him. He sat down at his desk with its beige phone with 12 lines and sold the whole lot of beef to Meatamation, an East Coast meat distributor, and its Connecticut salesman, Peter Matthew O'Donnell.

O'Donnell was on the phone to Vinnie Angus as the steer stepped from the truck into the tight steel coffin with the trapdoor floor.

A man wearing a white lab coat and dark plastic glasses reached down quickly and pressed a long tube against the steer's forehead and the animal was dead before the trapdoor dropped out and he rolled down to the big boys.

The big boys were the men who stood next to the conveyor belts. They could have been laying bricks or shoveling coal or making steel or spending eight hours a day, five days a week screwing one nut onto one bolt in some automobile factory, but instead, because of geography or family or desperation or dumb luck, they had wound up at the slaughterhouse, steeling themselves every day so they could go home and tell their friends, "Ahhh, it ain't so bad."

And after awhile, they started believing it themselves, so every day they could come in and stick a dead cow's back legs into a harness to be lifted up a shaft so that they, wrapped around in plastic and apron cocoons, could stick a knife in the cow's throat and rip it open up to the stomach so the steaming blood could pour out onto the floor, pushed by gravity and convulsing dying blood vessels.

Then they cut slowly around the head until it rocked easily and a final cut took it off. They stuck the head on another hook so a machine could rip off the skin with as little effort as a person pulling the plastic off an individually wrapped slice of cheese.

Then the skull would be steamed until the eyes cataracted and the exposed mess turned milky white. Meanwhile, the cow's body moved down to a man with hydraulic scissors who cut off the four hooves and dropped them into a hole in the floor. The carcass then gave up its final few drops of blood.

Further down the line, another big boy reached into the steer's belly and started hauling out the entrails, pulling them toward him like a large pot in a poker game, with both hands, then hurling them down a nearby chute.

Another machine peeled back the body skin until the meat-laden carcass was exposed. The trail then led into the freezer.

O'Donnell was talking to Vinnie.

"Big Vin, this is Pete."

"Yo, what have you got?" Vinnie's voice was a deep rumble, a vocal coal mine. He was only five feet eight inches tall, but everybody called him Big Vin because of his voice.

"I got what you want."

O'Donnell's home life was not all it could be. He was divorced, his kids did not like to talk to him, his ex-wife did not like to talk to him, so he enjoyed stretching out conversations before coming to the point. Which made everyone else not like to talk to him.

"What do I want?" asked Angus, noisily nursing his second beer of the morning.

"What do you need?"

"Two tons of rib, two of shoulder, two of flank, two of shank. Thin skin, no dirt under the skirt."

"Can deliver, except the shank. Can do one of shank."

"I need two."

"Don't do it. Shank is dying. I can get you one of shank."

"Two," said Angus.

"Shank is looking up a dead cow's heinie, for God's sake. Nada. One ton."

Big Vin barked out a laugh which sounded like an ax rebounding off a petrified tree.

"Never mind, skip the shank," he said. "I'll take the rest."

"Two rib, two shoulder, two flank," said O'Donnell, writing it down.

Vinnie Angus hung up without any further discussion of shank.

By the time he hung up, his last piece of meat had already been sectioned in the Houston freezer by a man so used to seeing his breath form a white cloud in front of him that driving home at night, it took him a few minutes to get over the fear that maybe he was dying because he couldn't see his breath.

The man made six uniform cuts into the body of the steer, then passed it down to a sallow-looking man who poked at it, peeled back an occasional layer of fat, felt along the rib cage, all the while moving quickly from foot to foot.

Finally satisfied with the quality of the cuts, he took a roller stamp and smacked purple United States Department of Agriculture insignias all over the cut-up carcass.

———

Two weeks later, Vinnie Angus left his wood-paneled, windowless office in the basement of his split-level home in Woodbridge, Connecticut, and got into his Monte Carlo sedan, the one he hoped he still had the good taste to hate.

His wife had harangued him into buying it to show their neighbors the higher status they had achieved by opening the second Vinnie's Steak House in Milford, just before the West Haven town line.

Before the Monte Carlo, there had been the swimming pool and the split-rail fencing all around their home and a gigantic station wagon and professional landscaping. All for status.

"What is this status thing that keeps eating at you?" Vinnie asked his wife. "Status? I sell steaks and hamburgers."

"Stop it, Vincent," his wife said. Her mouth puckered up. "You make it sound as if you were running McDonald's."

"If I was really making it, I'd be McDonald's. I'm not that good, so I run Vinnie's Steak House. So come off all this status thing, will you. I'm not made out of money."

"Is it that you don't have it, or you just don't wish to spend it on me and the girls? You always seem to have enough money for what you want, though. Those hunting trips. I've never heard you put one off because you didn't have the money."

"It costs me a tank of gas to go hunting, for Christ's sakes. What do you spend hunting?" asked Vinnie.

"Not much more than you spend around here on us, I guess," his wife said, her voice biting.

"Ah, stuff it. Buy what you want," Vinnie said. And she had. And the latest was this pussy car Monte Carlo that he hated.

His mood improved as he drove away from the house. He could mock his wife's insistence on status, but Vinnie Angus had come a long way from dishwasher in a greasy spoon in South Boston, where success

4

meant not getting killed by getting in between the blacks and the Irish who kept trying to murder each other.

He had watched and learned and saved his money, then made the jump to his own restaurant in New Haven. Everyone said that a good steakhouse could not be successful in a college town. Vinnie had made it work. He got the restaurant rolling and married the cute, leggy Jewish chick behind the cash register and moved into the suburbs.

His good mood went as fast as it had come.

What had it all gotten him? A too-big house with a too-big mortgage. A wife who covered her age with so much makeup that he had not seen the skin of her face in 10 years. A pair of daughters who were God's gifts to the orthodontics profession. And this gas-guzzling pussy car that he hated.

He had two restaurants, both successful, but the government and rising prices took out the money faster than his customers could put it in. Yet what else could he do but keep doing what he had always done? A failure, it occurred to him, could stop anywhere and start over, but a success was doomed to ride on the back of the tiger forever.

Vinnie Angus turned onto the Post Road and moved north, past the garbage antique shops, the railroad salvage stores, the tacky shoe stores, all the colored lights, the sparkling signs, the neon, the plastic, and turned left into his parking lot.

The warm gray-brown of his exterior wood visually softened the area. The muted lights glowing through the thick dark-yellow drapes gave the restaurant a glow even in the daytime.

When Vinnie Angus entered the restaurant, he forgot his problems. He was in another world, a world of his own creating.

Sitting on a crate in the simple cement block kitchen was his cook.

"It in yet?" Vinnie asked.

"Yeah," the cook said. "Just this morning."

The man got up and moved past Vinnie to the floor-to-ceiling refrigerator. He pulled out a slab of flank steak, sliced away at the outlying fat, poked it professionally a few times with a large two-pronged fork, then slapped it on the grill.

5

"Easy, you sucker," the cook said. He always talked to his meat.

"I'll be at the bar," Vinnie said.

Vinnie sat at the bar telling the bartender how he kept trying to teach grill jockeys that a good piece of meat was like a good whore. Slap her around a little and she'll get nice and soft for you. But beat the hell out of her and she'll be tough as nails.

"I hear you talking," said the bartender and poured another beer.

Twelve minutes later, the cook was out of the kitchen with a brown stoneware plate with beige trim clutched in a towel in his hand. Sitting in the middle of the dish was a dark, sparkling hunk of prime steak.

Vinnie cut into it, exposing a gray-orange plateau that seemed to suck at the blade of the knife.

"Nice," Vinnie commented. "Texture's good."

He sliced crossways with the serrated edge of the knife, then harpooned a piece with a thick silver fork the bartender laid in front of him. Vinnie plopped it into his mouth, ran his tongue across the outside for any sign of charcoal, then bit down.

The meat seemed to make way for his teeth until he got to the other side where, along the edge, it became tough and tinny for a microsecond, then seemed to melt and dissolve down his throat.

Except for that split second, it was the best flank steak Vinnie Angus had ever tasted. He finished it in seven big bites.

"There you go, sucker," said the cook to the empty plate on the way back to the kitchen. And Vinnie Angus went to his office to complain to Peter Matthew O'Donnell about the tinny taste around the government's USDA insignia.

"It's like eating goddam solder," Vinnie roared into the telephone.

"Easy, Big Vin. Easy. I'll light a fire under the ass of those Texas bastards. It won't happen again."

"Okay," said Vinnie Angus.

The Anguses had tuna casserole that night. Vinnie poked at three noodles, excused himself, then went upstairs to pack for his hunting trip the next day.

"Can hardly wait, can you?" said his wife in a tone somewhere between snide and shrill, from the other end of the table.

"Now, now," said Vinnie with practiced patience. He winked at his daughters as he disappeared out of the room.

Behind him he heard Rebecca, his younger daughter, say: "Do I have to? Daddy didn't."

"You want to look like him when you grow up? Eat," said Mrs. Angus.

And his older daughter, Victoria, said sharply, "Stop it, mother." He could hear her chair push back from the table.

Vinnie Angus sat down on the hard, thick wooden chair in his stuffy study. The chair creaked uncomfortably under the 20 pounds he had put on in the last five years.

He looked at his trophies and guns and looked forward to tomorrow. His throat would be scraped raw by the cold morning air. His breath would come in huge noisy gasps. His arms would grow tired from holding his twelve-gauge shotgun. His legs would ache by mid-morning. And he would love it. When he hunted, he was alone with himself, young again.

All he had to do now was to saddle soap his Timberline boots; make a lunch, pack his equipment, set his alarm clock for 4 A.M. and... He remembered one more thing he had to do. His monthly call.

He had been making them for eleven years, back since the time when the first Vinnie's Steak House had just opened and was floundering. The rich college kids had not yet discovered it and the visiting businessmen had not known it was there. Angus was desperate for money and the banks were not listening.

Then a Massachusetts friend had told him about a number he could call just to give information on the latest developments in the American meat industry. And Vinnie would get money for it.

By then, Vinnie would have separated his mother into cold cuts for cash, so he called.

A recorded voice told him to talk so he did, rambling on for 10 minutes on prices, stock, supply, preparation, control, and service. The recording asked him if he was finished, after a 10-second silence, then thanked him. Three days later in his mailbox, Vinnie found a postal money order for $500. With no return address.

When he tried calling back, the recording told him to return his call on the first of the month. And for 11 years, on the first of every month, Vinnie Angus called the number and rambled for cash.

He wasn't sure that he liked it but the 66,000 tax free dollars he was sure he liked. And what law could he be breaking?

Vinnie picked up the telephone, dialed the area code and seven-digit number, stuck the receiver between his jaw and shoulder, then started picking apart and cleaning his 9 mm sharpshooter's rifle.

The line rang twice before Vinnie heard a series of tonal clicks and then a monotone female voice said: "State name, address, zip code, and information please."

Vinnie was so anxious to get it over with that he did not recognize one more soft click as the upstairs extension phone was lifted.

"Supply has been steady," he said, "but it tapers off in different areas each month. This month it's shank. The quality of the meat itself is the best in years, so I'm expecting a price rise pretty soon.

"I've bitched to my distributor about the USDA markings being darker and deeper than usual. Today I bit into one and it was like eating tinfoil. We have to cut a little more of the fat to insure it all coming out."

Vinnie kept talking until he began to hear another conversation going on dimly in the background. At first he thought it was just a telephone echo, but then he was able to distinguish what was being said.

"Spock, this is no time for logic."

"Doctor, there is always time for logic."

"Are you saying, Mr. Spock, that Jim is lost out there somewhere and we are powerless to do anything about it?"

"It is a big galaxy, doctor."

Vinnie Angus quickly finished up. The recording thanked him, there were another series of clicks and the extension was broken.

"Viki?" he exploded. "Is that you?"

Far in the distance, he heard Captain James T. Kirk of the Starship *Enterprise* answer: "Warp Factor Eight. Now!"

"Viki? Are you there?"

His oldest daughter answered over the extension from upstairs. "Yes, Daddy. Who you talking to?"

"That's really none of your business, young lady," Vinnie said.

"Really, Daddy. I should think you would be much more respectful to this quadrant's representative from the United Federation of Planets. You're not doing much for intergalactic cooperation."

Vinnie Angus shook his head, despite the fact that he could almost see the smile on his daughter's face over the telephone. She was obsessed. Her room was filled with posters of the Star Trek crew, models of the Starship *Enterprise*, the Star Trek technical manual at $6.95, the Star Trek Concordance at $6.95, the Star Trek Reader, $10 in hardcover, six dolls of the Star Trek crew and one Klingon and cheap plastic replicas of the phaser, tricorder, and communicator.

"Try cooperating with this, Viki," Angus said. "I pay five thousand a semester to Yale so you can become a Trekkie?"

Victoria's voice lowered, conspiratorially. "You a spy, Daddy?"

"No. I've been doing this for years. For... for the Bureau of Agriculture."

"I never knew they had spies."

"Forget spies, will you. Here you are, 19 years old... "

"Almost 20."

"Almost 20 and you still play with Star Trek dolls. Stop it already. The show's been off for eight years."

"Nine," said Viki. "Do you know what those clicks were at the beginning and end of your call?"

"So they were taping the conversation. So what?"

"Not they, daddy. It."

"What?"

"You were talking to a computer, Daddy."

"So?"

"You don't get it, do you?"

"No," Vinnie shouted. "And I want you to forget it. You didn't hear that phone call, you don't remember it, and you won't mention it to anybody. Even your mother. Especially your mother. You understand?"

"I'm not a child, Daddy."

"As long as you love a man with pointed ears and green skin, you're a child."

Viki giggled. "Whatever you say, Daddy." She hung up.

Vinnie Angus smiled in spite of himself, thinking of the big luscious girl in tight jeans and sweater and harboring the strong suspicion that she had outgrown Star Trek a year earlier but still played at it just to annoy him. Why not? Daughters had done stranger things.

Vinnie finished cleaning his weapons and after his wife had left the kitchen made two bologna-and-cheese sandwiches with pickles. He packed them in a bag with four cans of Uptown Soda, left out his red-and-black woolen hunting cap, and went to bed at 10.

The alarm buzzed at 3:58 A.M. His wife snored on as Vinnie slapped the buzzer off and got up quickly. He dressed rapidly, got his gear together, walked down the hall past Rebecca's room, the sewing room, Victoria's room, picked up his bag in the kitchen, went down the front steps, opened the garage door, started the Monte Carlo, drove off on his hunting trip, and never came back.

———

Parker Morgan, an old retired architect, was walking his dog, an old retired bloodhound, in the woods around his home.

He loved the trees in the winter, standing out starkly in the cold clear air. Morgan broke off a dead branch from a fallen limb and threw it with all his strength.

The dog puffed laboriously after the stick, up over a small rise and out of sight. Parker Morgan watched his own breath condense and soon the dog came back, the twig in his teeth, two white splashes of carbon dioxide puffing out his nostrils.

Morgan kneeled down and the dog planted his paws on the man's knee and stomach, waiting for the branch to be taken and thrown again. Morgan took the stick, stood up, and then frowned.

On his knee and stomach were two bright red pawprints. He looked at the dog who quivered with anticipation. The dog's four paws were red. The old architect examined the dog but could find no cut or injury.

"C'mon, boy, show me where the stick was."

He started moving up the hill, the dog dancing around his side.

Morgan stopped when the hard frozen ground gave way to a patch of cold, moist earth. He touched the ground. His fingertips came up red. He smelled, then touched his tongue to his fingers, hoping desperately for the taste of berries.

It was blood.

Parker Morgan stared at his hand. A small red drop splattered onto the bridge of his nose from above. He looked up in surprise, and saw trouser legs hanging down from the tree branch over his head. His eyes continued rising, until he stared into the empty sockets of the skeleton in bloody hunter's clothing.

America's quadrennial exercise in civility had just ended and the country had a new President.

All around Washington, D.C., the last few moments of the inaugural ceremonies were like a starter's pistol, marking the beginning of a string of parties that would culminate later that evening in a dozen or more formal balls.

But the new President of the United States was not yet party-bound. Instead, he sat in one of the private offices of the White House, facing the former President across a large wooden coffee table, sipping lukewarm coffee from a pair of white paper cups.

The new President was on the edge of his chair, uncomfortable because there were no aides or Secret Service men in the room. But the former President slouched back on the sofa, his feet crossed under the coffee table, his balding, moose-jawed head looking in repose for the first time the new President could remember.

"This office is yours now," the balding man said, bitterly munching a canned macaroon. "The world is yours now and you have to learn to use it."

The new President shifted a little bit, coughed, and said dully, "I'm gonna try my best." He had taken speech lessons once to get rid of the Southern accent but they hadn't taken and his speech still was marked by the soft slurred vowels of the South.

"I'm sure you will," the former President said. "We all do." He nonchalantly pulled his feet out from under the table to rest them on top of the wooden surface, but he caught the rim and overturned his container of coffee.

Some of the liquid splattered onto the rug from the table and the balding man knelt down by the couch and with his pocket handkerchief sopped up the coffee from the rug and then blotted the table dry. He threw the handkerchief in a wastepaper basket.

"You know what's going to be the nicest thing about not being President any more? It's moving into a different house where we're going to have linoleum on the floor and washable indoor-outdoor carpeting, so when I spill a frigging cup of coffee, it can be wiped up with a paper towel, and I don't have to worry about some commission telling me 10 years later that I destroyed a national rug treasure."

"I guess you didn't ask me here to talk about rugs," the new President said.

"Very perceptive," the older man said drily. "No, I didn't. You remember, in one of our debates, I said the President had to keep options open. Because he was the only one with all the information available to him?"

"What debate?" asked the new President.

"What the hell difference does it make? I don't know. The one where I made the stupid mistake and you spent all your time not answering questions. Anyway it doesn't matter. I asked to meet with you now to give you some of that inside information that only the President knows. Some of the duties of the job that you won't find out about listening to Congress or the *New York Times*, the bastards."

The new President sank back into the soft chair. He nodded. "Yes sir, I'm listening."

"Do you remember that convention that had all those people killed in Pennsylvania?" The former President waited for a nod. "Well, there was never any question about what killed them. They were poisoned."

"Poisoned? By whom?" asked the new President.

"I'll get to that. They weren't the first cases either, but they were the most serious ones. Before that, for months, we were picking up reports of big groups of people getting sick. A party here. A wedding reception there. A church outing. Well, we put the medical boys on it right away, and they nailed it down quickly. It was poison. But the problem was that they didn't know what kind of poison or how it was administered."

"Why was nothing ever said about this?" asked the new President. "I don't remember ever reading..."

"Because you can't run the government of 220 million people out on Page One. Not unless you're willing to risk wild panic that you can't control. What do you do? Tell millions of people that someone out there's trying to poison all of you but we don't know who or how or why, now go to sleep and don't worry about it? You can't do that. Not and try to find any answers to those questions. Just listen, will you please? So there were all those poisonings but nobody died and it didn't seem like the end of the world when our guys couldn't find out the cause of the poison. And then came that business in Philly and all those people dead. And that made it something else. More serious."

"I'm surprised at you. I was briefed by the FBI and the CIA and all the federal agencies and departments and I was never told a word of this," the new President sniffed. "I'm surprised they withheld it from me."

"They didn't withhold anything. They just didn't know about it was all. Now let me finish. So after all the deaths in Pennsylvania, we had scientists come up with a vaccine that could offset the poison."

"Well, why haven't you given it to the American people? I can't understand any of this. This delay. This deception."

"We tried to give it to all the American people. Remember the swine-flu program?"

The new President nodded.

"Well, there's no such thing as swine flu. We invented that just to have a reason to inoculate the whole country against this poison. And then the goddam press shot down the swine-flu program with their harping about a few meaningless statistical deaths. So our asses are back in the sling." The big balding man rubbed his hand over the top of his head and scratched himself behind the right ear.

"Well, then make it mandatory that everyone gets a shot," the new President said. "Put it into law."

The ex-President smiled thinly. "Can you imagine the roar about trampled rights? After Watergate? The lawyers would break down our doors and string us all up as fascists. And I just don't think you can go ahead and tell the American people that there's a deadly poison somewhere in their food chain and we don't know where it is. Especially since there haven't been any more deaths since that convention. Maybe whatever it was passed off, and it's over now."

The smaller Southerner looked trapped in his chair, as if the full responsibility of his job was weighing on him for the very first time.

"What do we do?" he asked.

"What do *you* do?" answered the ex-President. "You're the President now."

"One thing I don't understand. A minute ago, you said the FBI, nobody, knew anything about this. How'd you manage that?"

"I was just coming to that. Take a tight grip on your cup and let me fill you in."

The balding politician sat back and began to tell the new President about a secret government organization named CURE, begun back in the early 1960s to fight corruption and crime, outside of the Constitution, before corruption and crime destroyed the Constitution.

Only the Presidents of the United States knew of the organization that was so set up that it did not even take orders from the President. The President could suggest assignments but CURE did its own thing.

"You've got no controls on it then," said the new President.

"You've got the ultimate hammer," the balding man said. "Tell it to disband and it disbands. Gone, forgotten and no one ever knows it was there." And the ex-President continued, telling how the organization had always been headed by a Dr. Harold W. Smith. And only Smith and one other man, their enforcement arm, knew what the organization did.

"Who's this enforcement arm?"

"I don't know," the President said. "I met him once. A surly looking thing. I don't know his name. His code's The Destroyer."

The new President had begun shaking his head as if grieving over what the older man had told him.

"What's all that cluck-clucking for?" asked the ex-President.

"It's true. I always knew it was true. There's a secret damned government in this country, secret intelligence people running around, trampling civil rights, abusing law-abiding Americans, and I'm just not going to have it. I wasn't elected to tolerate that kind of thing."

"You weren't elected either to tell the American people that someone is trying to poison them but you don't know who or why but tune in tomorrow and you'll keep them posted. When 30 of our best European spies get killed by the Russians inside four days and we're left defenseless in Europe, well, maybe you'll just want to tell the American people all about it. My decision was to respond in kind. I called this organization CURE and let them handle it." He stood up and smiled down at the smaller man. "You know, it's not really a matter of integrity. It's a matter of intelligence. Of running the country the best way you can for the largest number of people. CURE can help you. But you do what you want to do. If you want them to get off this poisoning business, that's up to you. All you've got to do is tell them to disband. Of course, if the deaths start up again next week, I don't know who you'll turn to then." He smiled sadly. "Because that's the first thing you're going to learn in this job. When the shit hits the fan, you're alone. Your cabinet, your family, your friends. Forget 'em. You're alone. CURE helps. But it's all up to you."

The ex-President walked to the door.

"I don't like it," the new President said. "I just don't like secrets."

"Do what you want. There's a red phone in the bottom right-hand drawer of that cabinet. Just pick it up. They'll answer."

He opened the door to the hallway, then turned around and let his gaze run around the room.

"This is your office now. Enjoy it. And do the best job you can."

Then he turned his back and walked out into the hall, closing the door behind him.

The Southerner stood up and walked around the room nervously rubbing his hands together. But each circuit of the office brought him closer and closer to the cabinet that held the phone and finally he stopped, opened the bottom right-hand drawer, reached in, and lifted the red telephone without a dial.

As the telephone reached his ear, he heard a clear voice which he immediately categorized as lemony, say "Yes, Mr. President?" No hello, no question, no welcome. Just "Yes, Mr. President?"

The new President paused.

"About this poison thing," he said.

"Yes?"

The new President paused again. Then quickly, as if it could not be a mistake if spoken quickly, he said: "Keep on it."

"Yes, Mr. President."

The man with the lemony voice hung up. The new President looked at the telephone for a moment, then replaced the receiver on the cradle, and closed the drawer.

He looked around the office, then through the windows, out toward Pennsylvania Avenue.

As he walked toward the door, he allowed himself a comment on his newfound knowledge:

"Sheee-it."

CHAPTER TWO

HIS NAME WAS REMO and the drunk tank smelled. The stench of vomit and booze-breath and whisky-soaked clothing would have been enough to asphyxiate any normal man. So Remo closed down his nasal passages and breathed thinly and waited for his case to be called.

The cops in Tucston, North Dakota, had found him wandering down the middle of the street wearing a black T shirt and black slacks, ripping the hubcaps off cars, and singing *Blowing in the Wind*. When they shoved him into the back of the squad car, they failed to notice that he wasn't shivering, even though he was only lightly clothed and the temperature was fourteen below zero, Fahrenheit.

And Remo hadn't said anything. He had presented his New York identification listing him as Remo Boffer, former cab driver, and been booked and waited in his cell.

And waited.

And waited for Judge Dexter T. Ambrose Jr. — "Hanging Dexter," they called him. And they were right, just so long as the defendants before him weren't part of organized crime or well connected or had a buck. Because those people somehow found a softer, more gentle side of Dexter T. Ambrose Jr., whose steel and acid was reserved for the poor, the unrepresented, the flotsam that floated through his courtroom.

It was 9 A.M. Remo knew without looking at a watch, and his plane would be leaving in two hours, and he hated time pressure and he hated hurrying. He had spent most of the early part of last night trying to find Judge Ambrose, but had had no luck. The man wasn't home and wasn't at his mistress' house, and wasn't at any of his regular haunts, and Remo realized that the fastest way to find him was to present himself at Ambrose's regular court session in the morning.

He had been standing now for six hours, leaning against the cinderblock wall of the cell, ignoring the grunts, the belches, the attempts at conversation of the nine other drunks in the tank.

Most of them had slept it off by now and they were a contrite, dirty band as they waited for their day in court and their one-way ticket to the county jail.

One of them woke up yelling. He was a big red-faced cowboy type in a yellow plaid shirt and jeans and a heavy hip length sheepskin coat. And when he had finished screaming his protest at the start of another day, he had struggled to his feet, looked around the cell, and marched upon Remo.

"You," he said. "Give me a cigarette."

"Don't smoke," Remo said.

"Then get one," the big cowpuncher said.

"Walk in the water until it covers your head," Remo said.

"Hold on a minute, skinny. You telling me you ain't giving me a cigarette?"

"I'm telling you I wouldn't give you a cigarette if I was P.J. Lorillard. Now go eat a cow."

"You too skinny a sumbitch to talk to me like that," the cowboy said, hitching up his belt.

"Right," Remo said.

"I'm too big to have to listen to that kind of crap from you."

"Right," Remo said. He heard footsteps coming down the stone corridor toward the cell.

"I'm gonna bust you up good."

"Sure. Swell, right, okay," Remo said.

The cowboy drew back his right arm and threw a punch at Remo's face. But the fist never landed. It found itself wrapped around by one of Remo's hands, and then there was pressure and the cowboy could feel the bones clicking, almost mechanically, as they were broken by the steady squeezing pressure of Remo's hand. Click, click, click came the fractures. The cowboy started to scream. Remo's other hand covered his mouth to silence the scream, then touched a clump of nerves on the left side of the man's neck, and the big cowboy slipped down on the floor, unconscious.

A policeman walked up to the front of the cell.

"All right, you stewbums," he said. "This is the order. Masterson, then Boffer, then Johnson…" he kept reading out all 10 names.

Remo walked to the front of the cell. "I'm Boffer. Take me first. Masterson's still sleeping it off."

He pointed to the big cowboy sprawled out on the floor.

The guard looked at the big man, then at his list, then nodded. "Okay. Let's go, Boffer. The judge doesn't like to be kept waiting."

"I wouldn't dream of it," Remo said.

The guard unlocked the cell, let Remo out, then carefully relocked the door behind him.

"This way," he said, and as he walked with Remo down the corridor, he asked, "You don't seem like the regular kind of drunk. What are you doing here?"

"Just lucky I guess," said Remo.

"If it makes you happy to be wise ass with me, you go ahead," the guard said, his feelings hurt. "But dontcha try that with the judge or you'll be spending the rest of the year making little ones out of big ones."

"Tough judge, huh?" asked Remo.

"The toughest."

"I always heard he was kind of easy on the big boys. You know, people with money to spread around."

The guard went on his defensive. "I wouldn't know anything about that."

"I would," Remo mumbled.

The court session, held in a high-ceilinged room on the second floor of the police station, was perfunctory. The two policemen stood before Judge Ambrose, a shiny-headed bald man with big shoulders and thick lips, and told how they had apprehended the perpetrator tearing hubcaps off cars on Madison Street at 3 A.M.

Judge Ambrose nodded. He looked at Remo with a measuring cold eye.

"Do you have anything to say before the court pronounces sentence?"

"Sure do, old buddy," said Remo.

He jauntily moved forward a few steps until he was standing right before the judge's bench. He reached into a vest pocket and drew out a small piece of paper and handed it up to the judge.

Judge Ambrose leaned over the paper as Remo moved back. The judge opened the paper. It was a note. It read: "Let's talk in your chambers."

Wrapped inside the note was a ten thousand dollar bill, the first one Judge Ambrose had ever seen.

Ambrose looked up and met Remo's eyes. The man's eyes were the blackest Ambrose had ever seen, almost as if they had no pupils.

The judge swallowed, then nodded. He crumpled up the paper and the bill and stuffed it into the pocket of his long judicial robe.

"I want to talk to this man in my chambers. Court is recessed for 15 minutes," he said.

"Twenty," said Remo.

"For 20 minutes," Judge Ambrose said.

Inside the judge's chambers, Ambrose sat behind his desk under an ornamental gem-cut crystal chandelier and looked across at Remo who sprawled in a leather lounge chair facing him.

"All right, Mr. Boffer. What's this all about?" he asked, waving the $10,000 bill at Remo.

"Call it survivor's benefits," Remo said.

"Survivor's benefits? I don't understand," Judge Ambrose said.

"You will," said Remo. "Nice chandelier."

"Thank you."

"That's the one you got free from Light City for deciding their way on a zoning case, right?"

"Who are you?"

"And the desk. That's from the Gilberstad Furniture Store, right? When you ruled that they could block the sidewalk for their annual sale days. And a kid walked in the street, got hit by a car, and died."

"I don't like the direction this discussion is taking," the judge said. "Who are you? Why should those things matter to you?"

"You don't know it, Judge, but you're part of a rich American tradition."

"Oh?"

"Right. Every year at this time, the organization I work for picks out the biggest penny-ante chiseler in the United States, and we do a thing with him."

"What kind of thing?" asked Judge Ambrose.

"Well, last year it was a zoning commissioner in Newark, New Jersey. We made him into a parking lot. And the year before that, a liquor-board investigator in Atlanta, Georgia. We drowned him in a vat of hooch from moonshiners he'd been protecting for years. And now, this year, it's your great privilege to join the ranks of the famous." Remo smiled, a nasty little thin-lipped smile that had no warmth and less humor.

"I think this interview is at an end," the judge said, standing behind his desk.

"I think you lose," Remo said. "Every year we get rid of one chiseler, just as an object lesson to all the other chiselers. Just to let them know that someone, somewhere is watching and someday it may be their turn in the barrel. This year it's yours."

Judge Dexter T. Ambrose Jr. opened his mouth to yell for the policemen he knew were standing outside the door to his chambers. But before a sound could come from his opened mouth, Remo had put a finger tight into the Judge's Adam's apple and the sound had sputtered and died.

"You'll never have a chance to tell anybody about this," said Remo from a spot next to the judge's left shoulder, "but you really ought to know why you're dying. You see, there's this organization called CURE and we fight evil."

He released the pressure on the judge's throat.

"But who are you?"

"I'm just your friendly old harbinger of spring, better times, and equal justice outside the law," said Remo, hardly moving but planting three stiff fingers into the exact point between the beginning of the judge's brain covering and the beginning of his face, creating a massive hairline fracture that splintered internally, down into the gray pulpy brain.

The judge nodded, seemed to sigh except no sound came out, flopped off his seat, given him in gratitude by the Aztec Furniture Company which had been given permission to erect a neon sign in a residential zone, and was obsolete before he hit the floor.

Remo carefully returned the $10,000 bill to his shirt pocket. Dr. Harold W. Smith, his boss, had a tendency to get upset when Remo left money lying around.

Remo looked around. There was no other door leading from the judge's chamber, except the one back into the courtroom, and Remo knew cops would be standing guard outside. Not that they could stop him, but they could force him into making a mess, and besides the policemen hadn't done anything wrong. No, the door was out.

So Remo opened the large window of the judge's second-floor office and stepped out. He dropped sharply for a few feet until he slapped back with his hands against the rough red brick of the courthouse building. His heels dug in and found a horizontal groove between the bricks and Remo stopped, leaning backward against the wall, suspended like a fly, and then slowly he let himself drift downward, concentrating on feeling the texture of the bricks under the palms of his hands, counting the grooves of the bricks with his heels, moving slowly until he was only a foot off the ground, and then stepping off the wall onto the sidewalk, as if the wall had been a small kitchen stepladder.

Tucston, North Dakota, was still too small to have traffic problems and Remo had no problem flagging down one of the town's three taxi cabs for the drive to the airport, and got there with plenty of time to spare.

Eight hours later Remo stood outside the New Haven Sheraton in Connecticut.

Just another hotel in a long line of hotels, motels, inns, guest rooms, and flophouses. Remo had left little bits of himself on registers all across the world.

Sometimes Remo Boffer, Remo Pelham, Remo Belknap, Remo Schwartz, Abraham Remo Lincoln. Even sometimes his real name, Remo Williams.

It didn't really make any difference anymore since he was dead.

Remo Williams had been dead since that hot Newark, New Jersey, night years before when a two-bit drug pusher was found mangled in an alley. The department had slapped a young rookie cop named Remo onto the train to prison and railroaded him to the electric chair.

It didn't make a difference that the chair didn't really work and Remo woke up afterwards in a sanitarium in Rye, New York. It didn't make a difference that he was to be trained as the enforcement arm of the super secret agency CURE. It didn't make a difference that he had become a more efficient killing machine than CURE ever had imagined.

None of those things mattered because what had once been Remo Williams had really died in that electric chair. Ten years of constant, bone-bruising, mind-stretching training had turned him into something else, something beyond human.

Remo had died so that Shiva, the Destroyer, could live. In the Hindu world, Shiva was the god of death and destruction. In Remo's world, the one man who counted thought that Remo was the reincarnation of that god.

Remo thought of this as he stood on the deserted, garbage-strewn New Haven street on the coldest evening of the year.

"Welcome home, Remo," he mumbled to himself. "Happy New Year."

Remo moved into the painfully lit, nearly empty lobby. He marched up the escalator, feeling the wide grooves through the thin soles of his black handmade loafers, to the mezzanine and the elevators.

He pressed the "up" button, went into a wide opening elevator, and rode up to the 19th floor, reading advertisements for the Tiki-Tiki Room, the Brunch Room, the Rib Room, and the Top of the 'Ton, which lined the opposed wall.

The doors opened smoothly onto the 19th floor and artificially chilled air, in which he could detect tiny residues of charcoal used in the filtration process, swept across his face like a plastic cloud. Remo allowed two long days to catch up with him and weigh his limbs down

WARREN MURPHY & RICHARD SAPIR

with the luxury of needing sleep. And with his training, that was all sleep was. A luxury.

He went to the door of his suite, which was never locked, and walked in.

A tiny, aged Oriental stood on a rice mat in the middle of the room holding several large pieces of parchment in his frail, long-nailed bony hands.

"What kept you? Must I do everything myself?"

"Sorry, Chiun," said Remo. "If I had known you were in a hurry, I would have run back from North Dakota."

"If you had, you would not have that stench of plastic airplane seats dripping from you." The little Oriental's hand swept the air in an arc. "Wash, then return, for I have a matter of the utmost urgency to discuss with you."

Remo willed himself to move wearily into the bathroom. He stopped at the door.

"What is it this time, Little Father? Another interruption of your soap operas? Barbra Streisand get a bad review? You have a Chinese bellboy? What?"

Chiun waved his hand again, like the swoop of a joyous dove before his face. A sign of indifferent patience.

"A Chinaman is just good enough to carry my trunks, although one must always watch them to be sure they do not steal the paint from the sides. Barbra Streisand's voice is still as clear as Korean sunlight and her beauty is unequalled. As for those other things you mentioned, they no longer warrant my attention."

Remo took a step back from the bathroom.

"Run that one by me again. I think it had something to do with your not watching soap operas anymore. Since when?"

"Since they have failed me," Chiun said. "Will you please wash the filth of plastic from your body? I will wait here for you."

Remo showered and when he came out of the bathroom wearing a knee-length cotton robe, Chiun was scrawling in Korean characters on the sheets of parchment.

"Now what's this about the soap operas?" asked Remo.

"They have turned to violence and have betrayed their own beauty. I have tried to stop this. I had you mail that letter to Norman Lear to warn him. Nothing has gotten better. Things have only declined." Chiun put down the feather pen and stared at Remo. "So I have written a daytime drama of my own." He waved the sheets of parchment. "You see it now, here before you."

Remo snickered. "You've written a soap opera?"

"I have written a daytime drama. That is correct."

Remo laughed aloud and fell back onto the sofa in the suite's living room. "Don't tell me. I know what you're going to call it. Rove of Rife. Right?"

Chiun transfixed him with a narrow stare. "Unlike some, I do not have any problem pronouncing R's and L's. If I had, how could I pronounce your names?"

Remo Williams nodded.

"For after all," Chiun continued, "cretin has an R in it and lunatic an L. To pronounce either wrong would be a disservice to your uniqueness as a semi human being."

Remo stopped laughing and sat up. "You set me up for that, Chiun."

"At last I have your attention. Now perhaps we may get down to business."

"Go ahead," Remo said sullenly.

"A daytime drama must be seen to be appreciated," Chiun said.

"Even to be believed," Remo mumbled.

"Silence. Now there are a number of ways to bring such a work of art to television. But since we do not own our own television station or manufacture baby food in small jars, we must find another way. Pay attention now, because this part concerns you."

"I can hardly wait."

"I have researched this question carefully and I find that writers who write things which find their way onto television share one thing in common."

"Besides talent?"

Chiun waved a hand as if to brush away the interruption. "They have agents. This is because of your mail system in this country."

"What does the post office have to do with it?"

"If a writer just put his story into the mail to send it to a television station, what would happen is what always happens to the mail. It would get lost, just as those lunatics have lost most of the mail that a faithful few have been sending to me for these years. So the writer gets an agent. This agent puts the story in an envelope and then he puts it under his arm and takes it to the television station and hands it to the proper people. This way it is not lost. Trust me, Remo, this is how it's done."

"That's not what an agent does," Remo said.

"That is just what an agent does," said Chiun. "Now for this, your professional agent gets 10 percent of what the writer gets. Because you are just a beginner I am willing to pay you five percent."

Remo shook his head, more in confusion than in rejection. "Now, Little Father, why did you pick me?"

"I told you. I have studied this carefully. You have the quality that is most necessary to being a successful agent."

"Yeah? What's that?"

"You have two first names." Remo looked stunned. "That is correct, Remo. All the big agents have two first names. Why this is I do not know, but it is so. You could look it up."

Remo opened his mouth to speak, then stopped. He opened his mouth again, then stopped.

"Good. You have nothing further to say. It is settled. Because I know you so well, Remo, it will not be necessary for you to have a legal contract drawn. I know you would never cheat me."

"Chiun, this is ridiculous."

"Do not feel inadequate. You will learn to deliver as well as any agent. I will help you."

Remo abandoned further protest as useless. "Well, we'll just stay loose on that for awhile. Now this soap opera of yours. What's it about? As if I didn't know."

"Ah, wait until you hear. It tells the story of this young, honest, noble brave man from…"

"…the village of Sinanju in North Korea," Remo said.

"…the village of Sinanju in North Korea," Chiun continued, as if he had not heard Remo. "And it follows this young man as he goes out into the cruel stupid world, plying his traditional art…"

"…of being an assassin like all the Masters of Sinanju," Remo said.

Chiun cleared his throat. "Plying his traditional art of personnel management, and how he is misunderstood and not appreciated, but he holds always true to his beliefs, and without fail sends gold back to his village, because it is a poor village…"

Remo interjected, "And without the gold, the people would starve and have to drown their babies in the bay because they couldn't feed them."

"Remo, have you been peeking at this manuscript of mine?"

"No, Little Father."

"Then let me finish. And our hero, older now, adopts a son of another race, but the son turns out to be a fat ingrate, who smells of plastic airplane seats and denies his father all good things." Chiun stopped.

"Well?" said Remo.

"Well, what?"

"How does it turn out? What happens to our hero and this ungrateful American son whose name probably turns out to be something like Remo Williams?"

"I have not yet written the ending," Chiun said.

"Why not?"

"I want to wait and see how good a job you do as my agent first," said Chiun.

Remo took a deep breath. "Chiun. I've got something to tell you and… and I'm glad the telephone is ringing because I won't have to tell you."

The caller was Dr. Harold W. Smith.

"Remo," he said. "I want you and Chiun to come to Woodbridge, Connecticut."

"Wait a minute. Don't you want to know how everything went in North Dakota?"

"It went fine. I heard about it. Did you bring back the $10,000?"

"I used it to tip the cabbie," Remo said.

"Please, Remo. Your attempts at humor are disconcerting."

"You think that's disconcerting, try this. I wasn't joking. He drove me to my hotel and didn't say one word. It was worth every penny of it."

"I'll pretend that I haven't heard any of that," Smith said in his dry, precise voice. "Woodbridge, Connecticut."

"Can it wait?"

"No. We are going to a funeral."

"Your treat or mine?"

"Be at the Gardner Cemetery at 7 A.M. And Remo?"

"Yes?"

"Bring the $10,000," Smith said, and hung up before Remo could tell him again, truthfully, that he had given it to a cab driver.

Remo replaced the receiver. Chiun was still standing motionless on the rice mats in the center of the room.

"And the title of this beautiful drama is…" Chiun began.

"Little Father, I've got bad news for you," Remo said.

"Oh. How does that make this day different from any other?"

"Your beautiful drama. I won't be able to deliver it right away, because I have another assignment from Smith."

Chiun rolled up the sheets of parchment. "That is all right," he said. "I can wait a day or two."

CHAPTER THREE

THE BODY OF VINCENT Anthony Angus was borne to its final rest in the Gardner Cemetery in Woodbridge, Connecticut, by a caravan of Cadillacs.

The long procession of shiny black cars passed through the heavy iron gates of the cemetery and past three men who stood in the early-morning chill near the cemetery's stone wall. Chiun wore a light-yellow robe, Remo a short-sleeved shirt and slacks. Dr. Harold Smith looked like a fuzzy gravestone, wearing a gray suit, gray overcoat, gray hat, and the grim gray pallor of a man whose universe is bounded by office walls.

Smith said hello to Remo and Chiun as they arrived.

Remo said, "Wait a minute," and unbuttoned Smith's topcoat. "Just checking," he said.

"Checking what?" asked Smith.

"Same suit, same vest, same white shirt, same stupid Dartmouth tie. I've got this picture in my mind of a closet filled with these same clothes and stretching on to eternity. And in the cellar of the White House, they have this laboratory and it's making dozens of windup Doctor Smiths to fill those clothes. And they're going to keep sending them out, sending them out, to order me around and around and around and..."

"You're very poetic this morning," Smith said. "You're also late."

WARREN MURPHY & RICHARD SAPIR

"I'm sorry. Chiun was busy rewriting his great new work."

Chiun stood behind Remo, his hands up the sleeves of his pale-yellow kimono, his sparse wisps of white hair blowing in the morning breeze like smoke.

"Good morning, Chiun," Smith said.

"Greetings, Emperor, who is as wise as he is generous. Your glory knows no bounds. Your telling will know no antiquity. Your wisdom will be spread on the sands of time forever. This humble thing shall earn your fame in Sinanju twenty-fold."

Smith cleared his throat. "Errr, yes. Of course," he said. He pulled Remo to the side. "He wants something from me. What does he want from me? I already send enough gold to that village of his to finance a small country. Now, that's it. No more raises in the tribute. I'll hire Cassius Muhammid to train you if he raises the price again."

"You don't have a thing to worry about, Smitty," said Remo. "He's not after your money."

"What then?"

"He thought with all your connections you might know somebody in the TV business."

"Why?"

"So you can help him get his soap opera on the air."

"Soap opera? What soap opera?"

"Chiun's written a soap opera," Remo explained happily. "It tells all about his life and career in America."

"His life and career?" Smith said. "It talks about us? About CURE?"

"Does it ever. But you really come off good, Smitty. Not penny-pinching or narrow-minded or anything. Just another big-hearted, friendly hirer of assassins."

"Oh, my god," Smith groaned. "Talk to him and find out how much he wants to throw it away."

"You're a philistine, Smitty. You'll never understand that us artists just can't be bought and sold that way. I'm surprised at you."

Smith sighed. "I'm not surprised at you. Not anymore. Not at anything."

"Anyway, Smitty. Just leave the whole thing to me. I'll take care of it for you. Now why did you bring us to a graveyard?"

Smith led them toward a slight rise in the ground. Down in a small hollow, a fat-faced minister, sweating despite the January chill, was mumbling prayers next to a casket, surrounded by two dozen persons.

"This is the funeral of Vincent Angus," Smith said. "He was one of our contacts in the meat industry. Of course, he didn't know he was reporting to us. Now we figure he was on to something because he was murdered. They found him dead in a tree. The flesh peeled off his body. That's why you're here."

"I didn't do it. I was in North Dakota," Remo said. He looked toward Chiun but the Oriental was listening to the prayers below.

"I know you didn't do it," Smith said. "Now this is complicated but pay attention. Someone has been trying to work out a way to introduce poison into America's food supply. That convention load of veterans at the hotel who all died. That was from the poison. Now under the guise of the swine-flu program we've managed to inoculate a lot of Americans, and we think the vaccine is 100 percent effective."

"So that solves your problem," Remo said.

"No, that doesn't solve our problem. One. We don't know if the vaccine is perfectly effective. Two. We can't give the vaccine to everybody because the swine-flu program's not mandatory."

"Why not?"

"Political reasons."

"Then let me talk to the politicians," Remo said.

"Remo," cautioned Smith.

"Ahhh, it's always like this, Smitty. I know what you're going to tell me. Find out who's doing the poisoning and stop them. That's always how it is. Find this and find that and find out how it works and find out how to stop it. I'm an assassin, not a scientist. Can't you just aim me at somebody?" He looked around for support to Chiun, but Chiun had drifted down the hillside and was now standing among the band of mourners, listening to the booming voice of the Rev. Titus Murray, whose three chins bobbed with the effort.

"And so we say farewell to Vincent Anthony Angus, good husband, father, skilled craftsman. A boon to his community, his family, and his church."

Rev. Murray took a moment to compose himself and wiped his face with a handkerchief.

"Rest in peace," he finished. "May God have mercy on your soul."

"What did this guy tell you before he got killed?" asked Remo.

"He reported a shortage of flank beef."

"Oh, well. That explains it. The giant flank cartel had to silence him before their secret got out."

"And he complained about the Department of Agriculture stamp on the meat in his restaurant. Said it was too thick and tinny tasting. I reviewed the tape last night."

"That's no help," Remo said. "Where'd he get the meat from?"

"Meatamation Industries. A salesman named O'Donnell."

"Okay. We'll see about him," Remo said.

He looked up to see Chiun coming up the hill with an attractive dark-haired girl in a long black dress.

Chiun bowed to Smith. "Emperor, knowing your great interest in this matter, I have arranged for this child to tell you all about the death of this poor man."

Smith looked shocked.

The young woman spoke. "I'm Victoria Angus. Are you really an emperor?"

Smith sputtered. "Chiun, did you... have you...?"

Chiun raised a consoling hand. "You need not worry yourself. I have told her nothing about your secret duties in Rye, New York, or the roles that Remo and I play in your plan to make America a better nation. Perhaps someday you can do me a favor in return."

"Report regularly," Smith said. He walked rapidly away.

"He's a very strange emperor," Viki Angus said.

"He can't stand funerals," said Remo.

"What's your name?" the woman asked.

"Remo."

"Remo what?"

"That's right. Remo Watt. Chiun you already know."

"Yes. Were you friends of my father's?"

"Associates," Remo said.

"You don't look like people in the meat business," said Viki.

"Well, actually we work with O'Donnell. At Meatamation?"

"Oh, yeah. The salesman. Surprised he wasn't here."

"He and your father were close, I understand," said Remo.

"Close enough so he should have come to the funeral." She looked at

Smith's figure walking briskly away across the cold dead-grassed surface of the cemetery. "Will he be coming to the house? Mr... what's his name?"

"Jones," said Remo.

"Smith," said Chiun.

"Mr. Smith. Will he be coming to the house?"

"I don't think so," Remo said. "He can't stand parties any more than funerals."

But Viki Angus was not really listening. She was thinking about her father's final phone call and the computer that answered. These three men might have something to do with that computer.

The man called Smith might be the brains, this Remo the muscle, and the Oriental... well, the Oriental could wait for classification.

They could be the "Bureau of Agriculture" men. They might be the men who murdered her father.

Viki Angus decided to call the father's reporting number and record the computer clicks.

Then she would break the clicks down into their unique computer code.

Then she would trace the code.

Then she would find the computer's central location.

Then she would find out who ran it.

And then she would kill him. Or them.

CHAPTER FOUR

Mrs. RUTH ANGUS WAS MOVING uncertainly around the house with her dusting cloth when the doorbell rang.

Mourners already?

She casually tossed the dust rag behind a potted plant and moved toward the basement playroom to reassure herself that the hors d'oeuvres were ready and the punch indeed mixed.

A cluster of liquor bottles and soda mixes was on the table next to the punch bowl and Mrs. Angus nodded in satisfaction. Just as well. If their friends were half as shaken as she by Vinnie's horrible murder, they would want their refreshments as powerful as possible. She herself had sneaked four fingers of scotch along with her Valium.

The doorbell rang again and Ruth Angus checked her coiffure on the stair mirror. She touched a curl here and a wave there, smoothed her long black dress, then leaned closer to see if the tracks of her tears through her heavy paste makeup were still visible.

Good, she thought, and went to the door. She turned the big copper knob which always seemed to give guests difficulty and pulled open the heavy wooden door.

Outside the screen door with the sheet metal "A" cutting across the lower panel were six Oriental men in long red robes.

Mrs. Angus gulped again and tried to stifle a light-headed giggle.

"Hello," she said.

The Orientals did not speak.

"Are you friends of my hus... my late husband's?" she asked lightly, but with, hopefully, the proper solemn tone for the occasion.

Five yellow men in the red robes remained motionless, but the man at the head of the group slowly nodded yes. Then he too joined the ranks of the motionless.

"Well," said Mrs. Angus, wondering about her late husband's taste in friends, "come in."

That got a reaction from the group. The two in back moved their heads quickly from side to side, as if surveying the neighborhood.

Mrs. Angus hoped they were not thinking of moving in, even with the two green-and-brown houses at the end of the block up for sale. The Ladies' Alliance for Woodbridge Neighborhoods, also known as L.A.W.N., had done much to insure that the West Haven blacks would not buy property piecemeal. And she was sure they would not like to start the whole process over again with Orientals.

The man in front smiled serenely. When his right hand appeared to pull open the screen door, Mrs. Angus noticed his fingernail.

It was at least three inches long, slightly curved, shiny, and cut at the end on a diagonal, like the blade of a guillotine. Mrs. Angus found it unnerving.

The six Orientals came in, crowding the foyer, each smiling appreciatively as they passed. The leader of the group, holding the door, entered last. He said, "How nice of you to let us in. We could not have entered otherwise."

Mrs. Angus heard one of the Orientals laugh. She thought it a strange way to say hello, but ignored the awkwardness of the situation. The Valium and four glasses of uncut punch helped.

"Won't you come downstairs?" she politely inquired, unable to spot any space between the six huddled bodies.

The men smiled even more broadly and began to move down into the playroom. Somehow, their moving made Mrs. Angus feel more comfortable.

She followed them into the playroom turned wake-room. The

group had gathered in a tight pack in the center of the floor. Their long red robes and dark yellow faces made her think of a bunch of life-sized lollipops. Mrs. Angus moved to the punch bowl to pour herself another drink.

"Help yourselves," she said, waving her arm to take in the rolled up salami and olives, the tiny tuna fish on white quarters, the bacon rolled around liver, the plates of ham and cheese, and the jello molds.

She could have sworn that the head man was scowling before she said, "It was a terrible thing. What happened to my husband, I mean. Over and over, I ask myself, why him? Why him?"

The head man caught her eyes with his own dark brown ones and said, unmoving, "At least he is free."

"Maybe," said Ruth Angus, gulping some punch before coming around the table, half-full cup in her hand. The punch definitely needed more vodka in it, she decided. She would spike it as soon as she had a chance. "Maybe. He doesn't have to worry about the mortgage and the taxes and all that stuff anymore. But what about me?"

She stood in front of the head man, swaying ever so slightly, and hid a slight burp behind her raised punch glass.

"What about me?" she repeated, her voice cracking this time. "What about the restaurants? The girls?"

Mrs. Angus considered the tile floor for a moment. There was no answer.

"Well, at least there's the insurance. There's that." Her fuzzy eyes moved up to the Oriental's dark ones. "But he was so young."

Her eyes clouded and tears began to cut new grooves in her cheeks. "I lived for that man. I honestly did. I lived for that man." Mrs. Angus sobbed and turned to refill her glass. Behind her was an Oriental.

She reconsidered the drink and moved to the right to sit down in the recliner for a moment. Beside her was another Oriental.

Mrs. Angus moved to the left to turn on the color TV set to get her mind off Vinnie's death. To her left stood a fourth Oriental.

She swayed forward. She felt the head man's outstretched hand steady her and take her punch glass. She half saw his long lacquered fingernail rising by her face.

"You lived for him," the man said. "Tell us what he said."

Mrs. Angus tried to focus her eyes but the man's face kept

expanding into a big yellow fuzzball. All she could really see clearly was his eyes. His dark, deep-brown eyes.

"When?" she asked uncertainly. "He said a lot of things. He said, 'What's for dinner.' He said, 'Shut up, I'm watching the game.' He said…"

"Before he went away," interrupted the Oriental. "Tell us what he told you before his hunting trip."

Mrs. Angus tried to slip between the man and the man on her left. She really wanted another drink. A fifth Oriental stood in her path.

"Lessee now," said Mrs. Angus. "I was reading before he went to bed, so he didn't say anything then. There was no ball game on that night so he didn't say anything then. He never watches 'Rhoda' so he didn't say anything then…"

The man in front of her gripped her shoulders and looked harder into her eyes.

"Vincent Angus' spirit is gone. It has been destroyed. His soul has been sent into eternity unfulfilled. His spirit shall never see the afterlife. He has died the Final Death."

A man behind her snickered.

Mrs. Angus began to cry again. She wanted to sink to the floor but the Oriental's strong hands kept her upright.

"I know, I know," she said. "He's dead. Poor Vinnie. What can I do?"

"Tell us what he told you. Reject all the falsehoods you have lived by. Reject Christianity. Reject meat. Bless the sacred…"

Mrs. Angus suddenly shook herself free with surprising wiry strength. She stumbled back into the chest of the Oriental behind her.

"Just a minute, buster," she said. "Reject what? Meat? Christianity? What are you talking about? I'm Jewish, for crying out loud."

She steadied herself. The man did not answer and her face began to crack again.

"Poor Vinnie. Do I need a drink."

A voice came from the front door at the top of the stairs. The man holding her shoulders turned to listen.

"She knows nothing," the voice called. "Get it over with. We have to get out of here soon."

Mrs. Angus had both hands up on the chest of the man behind her, politely asking if he would be so kind as to get out of her way.

The man nodded, but instead spun Mrs. Angus around to face the group's leader who swung his right arm across her neck, his forefinger slicing into her flesh.

Mrs. Angus only screamed once before the two Orientals beside her grabbed her wrists and the one behind her clapped his left hand over her mouth and used his right to cup her chin, pushing up.

The movement opened the three-inch-wide gash in her neck wider and a thin curtain of blood began to ooze down to her chest.

The head Oriental planted one hand on her shoulder and lanced his fingernail deep into the left side of her neck.

The tingling sensation exploded into searing pain for a moment as Mrs. Angus tried to scream again. The sound rose up her throat, but the yellow grip across her jaw only became stronger and the noise jangled across her tongue and died.

Slowly, the Oriental's finger, now touching her neck, his fingernail completely implanted, moved along his original incision. Blood began to pour out of the wound, founting out as much as six inches.

The pain was replaced by a nauseating sensation of drowning, as if her head were a cup being filled with liquid. Her face felt puffy and balloons filled her eyes, ears, and began to creep into her nose.

Mrs. Angus tried to pull herself above the water level, but the grips on her wrists kept her submerged. Her legs seemed like anchors and she felt a warm wetness move down her front. In another part of her mind she wondered what this wetness would do to the floor wax.

The Oriental's finger had reached the right side of Mrs. Angus' neck. He placed his other hand on her chin and pulled his fingernail out quickly. He looked at the weapon, then nodded.

The three Orientals released Ruth Angus and moved across to join their comrades on the other side of the room.

Mrs. Angus moved back, still on her feet and turned, hitting the table. Her upper body tipped sickeningly over the punch bowl.

Mrs. Angus saw the sparkling punch striped with several red strings before her eyes moved up into her lids and her body flopped back onto the wet tile floor. She never even understood that her throat had been cut.

The six Orientals waited until her body stopped moving, then began to edge forward.

"Let's get to work," said the leader. "We don't have much time."

Remo and Chiun drove Viki Angus home from the funeral. Actually, Remo drove since Chiun sat alone in the back seat of the rented automobile, scribbling furiously on a page of parchment with a feather pen.

"It's all so gross," Viki said.

"Yes, he is," Chiun agreed from the back seat.

"What's gross?" Remo asked.

"You are gross," said Chiun.

"I'm not talking to you, Chiun," Remo said. "What's gross, Viki?"

"The funeral. The whole thing. That fat faker of a reverend that my father hated standing there at the grave spilling out banalities. The whole awful murder. Why would someone, anyone kill my father that way? You have any idea?"

Remo put his hand comfortingly on her left knee. "Not idea one."

"Never ask that one for ideas, little girl," said Chiun. "He knows not the word."

"Come on, Chiun, knock off the carping, will you?" said Remo, turning onto the Angus' street. "What do you know anyway. You haven't been listening to anything that was said since we got to the cemetery."

"I know enough," said Chiun, his head still deep in parchment. "I know that the emperor has named a new disease after you."

Remo kept looking for the Angus house.

"A new disease? What's that mean?" he asked.

"Swine flu," said the small man from the back seat. He thought this line so funny that he giggled and repeated it. "Swine flu. Heh, heh, heh."

"Anyway," said Remo, "It's nice to see you in good humor and talking to me again."

"I am not talking to you. I am humiliating you."

Remo ignored him and turned back to Viki who sat looking out the window at her neighborhood.

"Why didn't your mother come to the funeral?" Remo asked.

"She was too torn up. She stayed home to get things ready for the wake. Here's the house."

Remo turned the rented car into the two-car driveway in front of the brown split-level with the yellow window shades.

As the three moved out of the car and up the lawn, Remo saw a dark figure moving alongside the house, bending over to peer in through a window.

"Wait here," he said to Viki. "Watch her, Chiun."

Viki moved close to Chiun as Remo moved off around the house. She put her hand on his arm and smiled at his impassive face.

"The man at the cemetery," she said, nodding toward Remo. "You call him emperor. Why?"

Chiun shrugged. "It is not for me to understand white men's games. I do not try. I call him emperor, Remo calls him Smith, the emperor calls Remo Nichols, everybody calls somebody something else. This is a very strange country but I will make it all clear when my beautiful drama is shown on television."

With that, the Master returned his gaze toward the house and remained silent. But his face had the same expressionless look as when he had stood next to the coffin in the cemetery.

Remo found the dark figure hunched over a cellar window a few feet ahead of him. Remo moved within an inch of the man. The figure rose and turned right into Remo's chest.

The Right Reverend Titus Murray almost had a massive coronary.

"Hello, Pastor," said Remo. "Trying to gain immaculate entrance?"

"Hugga, hugga, hugga," said the minister, back to the house, his belly moving like a bellows.

"Whatever you say," said Remo, taking Murray's arm and leading him to the front of the house. He waved Viki and Chiun up. "False alarm," he explained. "What are you doing here anyway, Reverend?"

Murray collected some of his composure. "Mrs. Angus didn't answer the door. I was looking for her. I thought she might need some spiritual comfort."

"Or help with the sandwiches from the looks of you," Remo said. "Viki, do you have a key?"

Viki bounced up the steps and tried the door. "That's odd. Mom never locked it before." She took a key from under the welcome mat and unlocked the door, then stepped inside.

Rev. Murray followed and Remo turned to Chiun who still stood on the front lawn, one sandaled foot poking the dead grass near the base of a tree.

"Come on in," Remo said.

"I think I will remain out here," Chiun said. "There is something here that I do not like."

"I know, me. Right?"

"This is serious, Remo. There is something here."

"Little Father," said Remo at the door. "It's cold and it looks like rain so come in."

"I will be out here," Chiun said stubbornly.

"Suit yourself," Remo said. He went inside and closed the door behind him.

Chiun waited a few seconds as if smelling the air, then began to move slowly toward the back of the house.

"There's food downstairs," said Viki, stepping up the stairs to the kitchen. "I'm going to wash my hands. Mom! I'm back."

Rev. Murray went downstairs and Remo stood in the foyer wondering what was on Chiun's mind. It was unusual for him to be so obviously worried about something, and when he was, it was generally serious.

Remo heard a soft hissing sound like the tiny wake of a miniature surfer from downstairs and then heard water begin to splash upstairs. Then Remo heard a harsh gasp from up in the kitchen and a thud from the basement.

Then he heard Rev. Murray's elephantine feet thudding upstairs, and then the minister ran by him, screaming, "Oh, God. Oh, God. Oh, God." His back was slick and red. Viki began screaming in the kitchen.

As Murray ran out the front door, Remo peeked down into the basement. The floor was covered with blood.

Rev. Murray had stopped next to a cypress tree on the front lawn and was throwing up.

Remo ran up the steps and into the kitchen. Soapy water was running down Viki's arms and face. She was standing straight, feet together, only occasionally bending her knees to gather air for another scream. There was no one else in the kitchen.

Viki's large brown eyes, now twice their normal size in shock, were looking over the sink, through the kitchen window, out at a carcass in a long black bloody dress who looked back from the limbs of a tree.

Remo leaned to the window and looked out at the remains of Ruth Angus.

And he saw Chiun, moving around the trunk of the tree, poking the cold winter ground with his toe.

CHAPTER FIVE

PETER MATTHEW O'DONNELL WAS ENJOYING a vodka and tonic in the comfort of his condominium apartment in the Timberwood complex of Westport, Connecticut, and watching the Vikings pretend to play in the Super Bowl when his foot became one with the ottoman.

One moment he was sitting before his color set with the newest electronic dial and the built-in recording unit, and the next moment the football game had become a jumbled haze and his foot had become part of the splintered wood, sharp-ended metal springs, screws, and stuffing.

O'Donnell tried to get up, but suddenly his other foot had joined the first and the bottom half of his legs were a foot stool.

"Time out," said a voice behind him.

O'Donnell lost his drink as well as his lunch, his breakfast, and part of his dinner the night before. His legs felt as if they had been used in the production of toothpicks and his bulky leisure shirt was a small green lake of evil-smelling liquid.

"Yaahaaa," he said.

"The score Anybody, 17, Vikings, zero," said the voice beside him. "You want to see the final score, you talk to me."

"Gaa gaa yaa haaa," said O'Donnell.

"Your name was on a small pad in Vinnie Angus' study. It said to call you. Why?"

"My legs, my legs."

"Right now they are," said the voice. "But if you don't answer me, your legs belong to me. I carry them out under my arm."

"He called to tell me that the meat I sold him has some tough spots."

"What spots?" asked the voice.

"Around the USDA mark."

O'Donnell saw a hand attached to a thick wrist move down his leg, slowly, like a pearl drifting through pancake syrup, and suddenly his left foot miraculously healed.

"Aaaaaahh," he said in satisfaction.

"Good. Now," said the voice, "why did he die after calling you?"

"I don't..." O'Donnell began to say and then there was a blur in front of him and his left leg felt as if it had split in half and re-wrapped itself in braids.

"Woo ha. Ya. Ya. Ya," O'Donnell said.

"Why?" repeated the voice.

O'Donnell's hands flew to his leg. They sank into the green goo that had seeped through his gray knit slacks.

Where was the greatly lauded security of this damned condominium park? Where were the cameras? The double-lock doors? The little guardhouse in the parking lot?

O'Donnell saw the thick wrist again move, this time toward his right leg.

"No, no," he shouted. "I'm not sure, but I think the meatpacker."

"Why?" The thick wrist moved away from his leg again.

"Because I told the packer and he was upset and he wanted to know if Vinnie had told anybody else." As he spoke, O'Donnell stared through pain-blurred eyes as a football announcer interviewed boys of nine, 10, 11, and 12 who were involved in a passing-and-kicking contest. O'Donnell thought the kids looked like whirlybirds in their outsized shoulder pads.

"And what'd you tell him?"

"I told him I didn't know. I didn't think so."

"All right. Who's the packer?"

"Texas Solly. Texas Solly Weinstein in Houston. I called him and told him. That's the truth. I swear." If O'Donnell ever got hold of his real-estate agent, he'd ram all of the Timberwood condominium's security devices down his throat.

"What's Solly's number?"

"It's at my office. At Meatamation."

The thick wrist moved again toward his leg.

"No, no. Honest. I don't carry his number. I just punch out a coded number on my line and it connects."

"What's the coded number?"

"I punch out four-oh-seven-seven," said O'Donnell, staring at the big white numbers on the red jerseys of the kids until the red washed over the white and the famed Triquinox color turned to an inky black. The set stayed on but he turned off and passed out.

Remo wiped the small flecks of bile from his hand onto O'Donnell's shirt, then looked up as Chiun entered the room.

"You must not go any farther," said Chiun. "Stay here."

"Since when do you like football?"

"Do not go," Chiun repeated.

"Sorry, Chiun. A job's a job."

"Then we will both go." Remo looked up. "We will both go and I will tell you of the skeleton in the tree and what it signifies and then we will tell Emperor Smith that we do not like this assignment and will not do it."

"He'll really be happy to hear that," said Remo. "Somebody's trying to poison all America and we're going on vacation."

"Americans have been filling themselves with poison for years," Chiun said. "It is in their food, it is in their air. They smoke poison. They ride in poison. They replace milk with poisonous chemicals. If they did not want to die, they would not do it. So why should we stand in their way?"

Remo would have argued if he could have seen any flaw in Chiun's reasoning, but he couldn't. So he said, "We go."

And Chiun said: "This is a bad thing you do, more bad than you know."

The Meatamation office building and distribution center sat on the lovely Westport countryside like a castaway egg crate. It was one of the new gray architectural wonders that clashed with nature and reveled in wasted space.

Remo stopped in the main driveway when he saw a pack of screaming people marching back and forth in front of the building's main entrance, a great hulking swaying mass, waving signs and shouting.

"I will stay here," Chiun said. "These noise-mongers offend me."

Remo found a gray-haired man in Levi's and gold windbreaker watching the people march.

"You work here?" Remo said.

The man nodded.

"Where's O'Donnell's office?"

"Who?"

"Peter Matthew O'Donnell."

"Why do you want to see him?" the man asked.

"I'm his sister. Mother is ill," Remo said.

"I guess it's important."

"Yeah."

"It'll be tough getting in there today," said the gray-haired man, nodding his head toward the marchers.

"Just tell me where O'Donnell's office is. I'll worry about getting in."

"I don't know O'Donnell. Never heard of the man. How should I know where his office is? You could ask the guard inside."

"Go pound sand," Remo said. He started moving toward the door.

"Be careful," said the man. "Don't make them think you work here."

Remo stopped. "Why not?"

"I don't know. They're yelling something about not wanting scabs."

"They slow me down, they're going to have plenty of them."

When he got close to the line, a bland-faced middle-aged woman in knee warmers, long fur coat, knitted scarf and mittens turned toward him and started screaming, "Pig, swine, fascist butcher."

Remo smiled pleasantly and kept moving.

A man in a knitted woolen cap and pea coat stopped and pushed his sign close to Remo's face. Remo plucked out the two nails holding the placard to the post and walked on. The sign flopped to the ground as

Remo sidestepped a young mother screaming at her nine-year-old son to bite him on the leg.

Finally Remo got to the door. An overweight black guard on the other side of the glass, who had no gun, no nightstick, and probably no dimes to use the lobby pay telephone, desperately motioned for him to go away.

The back of Remo's neck was accosted by hot breath. He turned to face a half-dozen aggravated people pressing in on him waving their signs menacingly.

Remo was considering the possibility of laminating them to their signs when a voice rang out: "Back off! Back off!"

The group stopped a few inches from Remo, then turned, grumbling, and walked back to their picket lines, making way for a young, auburn-haired girl in tight-thighed bell-bottom jeans and a multicolored knit sweater. She stalked over to Remo, stopped, put one hand on her hip, and stamped her foot.

"Well?" she demanded.

"Not bad," Remo admitted. "On a scale of one to 10, I'd give you an eight and a half."

The green eyes of the auburn-haired girl flashed.

"What do you think you're doing?" she said.

"What do you think *you're* doing?"

"We are helping the helpless. We are defending the poor. We are protecting the downtrodden. We are fighting for ignored rights."

"You're doing all that? Here? At a glorified butcher shop?" asked Remo in wonder.

Another chorus of chanting filtered through their conversation.

"We are marching for the Third World," the young woman said. "The Third World is poverty. The Third World is hunger. The Third World is two billion people going to bed at night with empty bellies."

Remo shrugged. "The Third World is two billion lazy retards and 2,000 big-mouthed liberals. Save 'em if you want. But why at a meat factory?"

"Look at you," the redhead said. "You've never known hunger." She looked at him more closely. "Well, maybe you have. Maybe a little bit. But probably a self-imposed hunger to conform to a corrupted society's standard of beauty."

Remo noticed that the girl seemed to take pains that she herself matched that corrupt standard of beauty. Every curve, every line of her body was just the right size and shape and in just the right place.

"Do you hear what those people are saying?" she asked.

"No," said Remo. "I can't make it out."

The redhead stamped her foot again. "They are crying out against this capitalist society's attempt to crucify us all on a cross of meat. They are shouting, we'll eat no more meat. We'll take no swine-flu shots."

The girl broke off her conversation to scream out the message with the rest of the group a few times. Then she turned back to Remo.

"This is a joke, right?" Remo asked. "You're all really members of The Movement of the Month Club, right?"

"Our aim," the girl said haughtily, "is to convince this corrupt government that America has a moral obligation to feed the rest of the world."

"I doubt that the rest of the world will stop breeding long enough to eat," Remo said. "What does that have to do with swine-flu shots?"

"The answer is not shots," said the girl. "It is to stop raising and eating swine. It is to stop wasting millions of tons of grain fattening steers so that we can eat meat. Do you understand now?"

"No," said Remo.

"Why should you?" the girl said. "You work for this decadent company. Well, we're going to shut it down. Tight. And after this one, others. All across the country, until this nation comes to its senses. What's your name?"

"Remo Nichols," said Remo, watching the black guard trying to fit pennies into the pay phone.

"I'm Mary Beriberi Greenscab. I wouldn't suggest trying to get in, if that's what you're thinking of."

"Mary Beriberi Greenscab?"

"Short for Marion. You want to know what my name means?"

"Not right now," said Remo. "I'm planning on lunch soon."

"Beriberi is a deficiency disease marked by an inflammatory or degenerative change of the nerves, digestive system, or the heart, which means it usually causes a person to have fits, migraines, a bloated stomach, diarrhea, and heart attacks."

"That's nice," said Remo. "We'll have to talk again real soon." He saw that the guard had found a dime and was talking now on the telephone. The police would be here soon.

"And Greenscab signifies the micro-thin layer of algae that forms on the inside lining of the stomach just before starvation."

"Terrifically disgusting," Remo said. "If you'll excuse me…"

"If you try to get in," said Mary suddenly, "we will have to stop you."

"Stop away," said Remo, going for the door.

"I warn you. It'll be a shame to trample you."

"It's all right," said Remo, his hand on the lock of the glass door. "I'm a vegetarian. And I don't work here."

"I don't believe you," said Mary. She barked out, "Gotta scab here. Get him."

Just as Remo pressed the lock out of the glass and pushed open the door, the 24 picketers turned and charged as if they had been waiting for that command all day.

Remo saw the black guard blanch. Inside the door, Remo leaped up to the top of the entrance over the head of the crowd, and the protesters, eight feet wide at their narrowest point, hit the three-foot-wide entrance at a speed of 13 miles an hour. The splat and crunch were gratifying.

Remo hopped lightly down to the floor as the first groaning began. The guard had backed against the wall.

"I called the cops. You better get out of here. I called the cops."

Remo spotted O'Donnell's name and office number on the wall directory and ran off down the main hall, singing *Mary had a little lamb, little lamb, little lamb. Mary had a little lamb, its fleece was white as snow.*

The office door was locked. Remo popped it open and three Orientals stuck their hands in Remo's face. Or tried to, because just as the first fingernail reached the point where the air displaced by its movement slightly increased the pressure against Remo's skin, Remo moved instinctively.

His head moved across, his own hand fluttered out, and the first man became a wall fixture. Remo slid his body sideways into O'Donnell's office, his foot moving across at a sharp angle to his body, and because Remo wanted to save one of them, the second man found his first kneecap driven into his second kneecap, making jelly of both. The man crumbled, howling, to the floor as the third Oriental faced Remo and executed a perfect straight-arm karate thrust toward Remo's exposed neck.

Perfect, except Remo drove his own fingers like a wedge between the Oriental's fingers and through his radius and ulna, cracking the man's arm like a piece of kindling.

The shattering concussion exploded the Oriental back through the office window out onto the stone below, which he hit with a terminal thump. Remo turned just as the second man fell on his own upraised fingernail. His torso sank to the floor and began to leak blood onto the carpet.

It was only then that Remo noticed the length and sharpness of the Orientals' fingernails, as well as a paper-thin cut across the top of his right hand. Remo clenched his fist and watched a thin red line grow between his second and third finger. A tiny bead of blood crossed his wrist and disappeared into his shirt.

It had been so long since he had seen his own blood that the sight fascinated him. But a commotion out in the hall broke him out of his reverie.

Remo ran quickly behind O'Donnell's desk, picked up the telephone and jabbed the touch-tone numbers, four-oh-seven-seven.

Remo heard the line click three times, then a recorded voice said: "The number you have reached is not in service at this time. Please check your number to be sure you are dialing correctly. Thank you."

Then 24 meat protesters piled into the room.

CHAPTER SIX

THE POLICE, DEALING WITH THEIR first murder in 11 years, were really tough. They talked to all the picketers and looked at them real hard.

Every time one of the protesters would answer "why?" to a question, the policeman would say, "Do you want to go downtown?" and then the picketer would answer the question.

Except once, when a thin, tall, dark-haired, thick-wristed marcher asked "why?" and the cop said "Do you want to go downtown?" and the thick-wristed marcher said, "Is it nicer than uptown?"

"Don't get wise. Name?"

"Mine or yours?"

"Yours."

"Remo Nichols."

"Address?"

"Number 152 Main Street." There was always a 152 Main Street.

"Did you ever see, know, or kill the three alleged victims?"

"No."

"Who saw you not kill them?"

"Everybody. Nobody. I don't know what that question means," Remo said.

"Do you want to go downtown?"

"I did. I saw him," said Mary Beriberi Greenscab.

The policeman turned to her.

"What's your name?"

"Mary Beriberi Greenscab."

"Address?"

"Do you want to know what my name means?"

"Do you want to go downtown?"

Remo left the Westport Meatamation plant a free man. The police never called him back, deciding after intense discussion to call the three deaths a double-murder suicide resulting from an argument among the three Orientals.

Mary caught up with Remo near his car where Chiun still sat.

"It took you long enough. What happened to your hand?" Chiun asked.

Remo looked down at his right hand. Already the fingernail slice had become a dim pink line as Remo's body regenerated tissue to heal and restore itself.

"I was cut by a fast finger," Remo said.

Chiun stared at Mary. "What did you do wrong?" he asked Remo.

"I didn't do anything wrong. He was just faster than I expected was all."

"You assumed again," Chiun chided. "You assumed that you were dealing with less than yourself."

"Isn't everyone?" asked Remo.

"You are lucky it was not your throat that was cut," Chiun said petulantly.

Mary coughed quietly under Chiun's gaze and pulled a plastic packet out of her pocket and ripped it open with her teeth.

"Anybody want some caraway seeds in carob syrup?" she asked.

"I would as soon eat dirt," said Chiun evenly. "Remo, who is this canary who eats birdseed?"

"Be nice," said Remo. "Mary here helped me get out of the mess inside with the cops. And she's against meat and against swine-flu vaccine."

"The joy in my heart is boundless," said Chiun.

"Not nearly as boundless as it'll be when I tell you we're going to Houston."

Chiun nodded sadly. "And yet you pursue this mission, despite my warnings." He scrambled out of the car. "You will see before much longer."

Chiun turned and walked away, and Remo watched until Chiun moved over a slight hill, his kimono wafting behind him, his arms folded in front, making him look like a cone on wheels.

"One little cut and he goes all to pieces," muttered Remo. He turned to Mary who was sucking on the plastic. "Sorry about that."

Mary's head came up, bits of seed sticking to her lower lip. "Sure." She licked the seeds up, nodding toward the diminishing Chiun. "Friend of yours?"

"Relative," said Remo, beginning to move up the hill. "Thanks again."

"Anything for a fellow vegetarian," said Mary with a small smile. "See you around."

Remo moved to the top of the first hill in time to see Chiun disappear over the second. He upped his running speed and made it to the top of the second hill in time to see Chiun round a bend in the distance. Remo felt as if he was trapped in a nursery rhyme.

The bear went over the mountain and what do you think he saw? He saw another mountain. Remo went to the bend and saw Chiun pass through a bunch of trees. Remo went to the trees and saw Chiun move behind some rocks. Remo moved to the rocks and saw Chiun sitting on his bent knees 500 yards away.

Remo reached Chiun as evening descended. As he grew near he saw that the Korean had his hands deep into the hard, cold ground up to his wrists.

When Remo moved in front of him, Chiun lifted his arms and exposed a small hole filled with the gory remains of internal organs.

Remo recognized the heart and the liver before he looked up at Chiun. The old man raised one thin finger skyward. Remo looked up. Nestled in the crotch of a tree, silhouetted against the full moon, was a corpse in a bulky leisure shirt and gray double-knit slacks. All that was left of Peter Matthew O'Donnell.

"They always bury the organs near the base of the tree," said Chiun.

"Who are *they?*" asked Remo, looking at the red, lumpy underground soup.

Chiun stepped away from the tree and folded his hands in the flowing sleeves of his kimono. "They are, my son, as old as Sinanju itself," he said.

And Chiun spoke:

"The House of Sinanju is old but it was not always old. There is nothing that was not young some time. At this time of which I speak, the House of Sinanju was young. Pharaohs there were in Egypt and they knew of us. And the great emperors of China, they too knew of us. The Middle Kingdom had great respect for Sinanju. Before the horseman, Genghis Khan, this was. And we had great respect for the Middle Kingdom, too."

Remo nodded. As he had learned to memorize the names of the Masters of Sinanju, each with his special deed and special legend, there was always respect for this long succession of Chinese emperors of the Middle Kingdom, which spanned dynasties.

"The Master's name was Pak and we were young but respected. Pak was not as we know a Master of Sinanju to be, for then there were several masters and we had not yet achieved the sun source of the power of the body. It was a few centuries later that this happened under the greatest Master, Wang, of whom many took his name in later generations. Thus you should know who and when and not think one is another.

"It was a time, Remo, when Masters of Sinanju still clung to weapons of sharp iron," Chiun said.

"The old days, Little Father," said Remo smiling. He had seen for the first time on the magnificently serene face of Chiun the jarring discord of fear, and this moment, allowing Remo to interrupt without rebuke, was an echo of that terror.

Remo did not like that thing that dimmed the shiny thorny glory of Chiun, the Master of Sinanju, his teacher. That which made Chiun quiet in respect was an offense against Remo's life breath.

"There was an emperor," said Chiun "and this emperor said to his Master of Sinanju, 'There is a province' — near Shanghai, as it was later to be called — 'and there is a great forest and in this forest are knaves and disrespectful people who do not revere their emperor or the order of things.' The emperor said there had been demands for ransom for his governor of that province. And his answer, he said, was Sinanju."

Chiun nodded deeply, this nod meaning that the situation was established. It was the form of instruction by story of Sinanju. First where and what and when, then what ensued, and what the House of Sinanju learned from what ensued. The early lessons of the House of Sinanju were dear. They were bought at the price of lives.

"And Pak took with him man servants and handmaidens, the last master to take servants. And he came to that forest near Shanghai and he said to the dwellers therein that he was Pak and he had come from the emperor. And he would wait a day by this forest and woe unto them if they had not returned the emperor's governor to him."

"That night, two maidens were missing from Pak's camp, and Pak sent two man servants to find them. But only one of those man servants returned and he wailed that the Master of Sinanju had sent servants where he himself feared to go. And the man had no fear of Pak, for one of the maidens had been his own favorite daughter. And Pak said, 'Grieving father, it is right that you are angry and I have failed you for it is more important for a master to protect his servants than his own master. This is true virtue.' And he sent away all his servants and to this day we do not have servants," Chiun said.

"Okay. That solves Thursdays off," said Remo. "But what's all this about smoke and bodies in trees? I mean, what's the purpose of this story? I know we don't have servants because I usually end up carrying your trunks. What are you getting to?"

"A Master of Sinanju watching other masters die. Which was a good thing."

"A good thing?" asked Remo. He sat down on the ground and faced Chiun. "How can that be?"

"Because if Pak did not watch his brothers, his uncle, and his father die, we would not be here, nor would the House of Sinanju. Glory to Pak who could endure great wounds in the forest near what would one day be called Shanghai."

And Remo heard the gruesome tale. Pak went into the woods and saw why the servant had grieved. There was the delicate head of the girl at the foot of a tree and inside the hollowed trunk, the skeleton picked clean. And the organs were buried in a hole under the tree.

The face of the girl was white, "a pale disgusting death white," said Chiun. Remo shrugged.

"And Pak noticed smoke on a ridge and he wondered what was

burning and went to it and from the smoke he heard little cries of triumph and heard voices in the dialect of that region.

"And those who spoke had seen Pak's servants leave and they thought Pak had left, in retreat, and this saved his life, for they did not see him when he approached, because it is common knowledge that what you do not look for, you do not see.

"At that time, Pak knew stillness as did other masters and was still and the smoke moved past him and behind trees it formed. And Pak followed, now knowing what to be aware of, for this was a new thing, that people could be in smoke."

"Are we working with people who are in the smoke or what?" Remo asked. "Hidden by it?"

"The smoke is one form of the people," Chiun said.

"Now it is believed in the West that vampires suck blood from the throat but this is not so. It is a distortion from tales carried by Genghis Khan; and his farthest conquest into Europe was Eastern Europe where tales of vampires became well known.

"For the blood drinkers it was a religious ceremony. They did not eat meat but drank blood and this was done by opening the heart and suspending the blood-carrier over a giant copper vessel and he became disgustingly white."

"Enough on the disgusting white," Remo said.

"It is not I who made white the color of death," Chiun said. "It is nature."

Remo let it pass. Chiun went on to tell how first the men, then the male children, then the female children, and then the women drank from the blood in the pot. And the trunk of the body was boiled until the flesh and sinew were floating free. "And this was fed to the yapping dogs of the Shanghai forest.

"And Pak watched a tree being hollowed and the skeleton put into it and he learned that this was a gift to their ancestors. And Pak learned that these beasts believed their ancestors needed these offerings in the after-world and that someday there would be a great sacrifice to feed those many souls for all of time. And they looked forward to death.

"Pak continued to watch and when he failed to return an uncle who also served the court followed him. And Pak saw the smoke settle around the man's shoulders and he was about to warn his uncle, when the smoke spoke, and a voice said 'May we enter?' and the uncle, surprised, said 'Yes,' and the smoke became man and struck, these people even then having long killing nails.

"Yet the stroke was not as strong as their magic and it wounded the uncle who struck on an interior line, and, being Sinanju, dispatched immediately this blood-drinking vermin. But the next smoke came to the outside and made many killing blows in the neck.

"The next day two more figures came up the road and they were Pak's father and brother and they camped near the forest. Pak went to join them and told them what he had seen and suggested they, all three, fall on this band. But his father, Wang, not the great one, insisted that Pak watch as they attacked those in the smoke so that if they failed, he would know all the ways they use in killing, for this was the first step. What you know, you can kill. Now the outside attack is a circle and the inside is a line."

"Jesus Christ, Chiun. Who do you think I am?" asked Remo angrily.

"It never hurts to repeat basic wisdom."

"It gets tiresome in the repeating," said Remo.

"So Pak returned to the forest and the next day his father and his brother approached and they knew the smoke was dangerous, and one, very casually, as if he were practicing a stroke, moved his sword through the smoke and Sinanju discovered one did not kill these blood-drinkers when they were smoke.

"So they walked on farther and Pak saw great clouds of smoke form. And then in an instant there were seventeen of them and they taunted the Masters of Sinanju and said, 'Do you invite us in?' and the Masters nodded, and they attacked on the interior line with the finger and on the exterior with the sword. And Sinanju claimed ten, but we are assassins, not soldiers, and dying is no triumph nor does it feed the babies of Sinanju.

"And Pak now knew much of the way these blood-drinkers fought, but he thought there was more to learn. And he watched. But the next day, up the road came his only son and while with pain he had watched his uncle die and father die and brother die, he could not watch his son die.

"So to the center of these bloodsuckers went Pak and laughed and said he was a Master of Sinanju and they would meet their deaths now.

And they said they had killed Masters of Sinanju but Pak said they had only slain servants who had slain more of them. He said Sinanju knew all about them with their smoke and blood-drinking and he demanded they leave this forest and go live among the barbaric whites to the West or the animal blacks in the hot places.

"And this they did not accept, of course, and they fell upon him and he slew many, but they could only wound him. Pak kept life in him longer than it wanted to stay at great pain. And they believed they had failed against Pak, packed and took with them their copper pot and their weapons and left the forest and when they passed Pak's son, they bowed with respect, for Pak had told them the young one coming up the road was Sinanju also.

"What was gained there in the forests near what would be called Shanghai was the knowledge of the ways the bloodsuckers moved, how they killed and how they drank blood and disguised themselves as smoke and they could not kill unless they were invited in. And there was a truce."

This Chiun told Remo and it was thought that sometime during the ages, the bloodsuckers had died off.

Pak kept his life long enough to tell his son what Chiun had told Remo. And he told him something else. "That the bloodsuckers had no fear of death."

"We could give them a hell of a fight," said Remo.

"What is this?" shrieked Chiun. "Have I spent my years making a ballfoot player, a banger of sticks? You are an assassin. You are not an entertainer. Close is the same as never, you white dense mud-thick pig mind."

"I'm sorry," said Remo.

"You should be. And now we face these bloodsuckers again. And they have ways to kill we may not yet know of."

"We'll do the best we can. We just won't invite them in. By the way, what happened to the emperor's governor? The one Pak was sent to rescue?"

Chiun shrugged. How should he know? "Who keeps track of Chinamen? They are so many."

Victoria Virginia Angus sat at the Honeywell computer console with the ITT extension phone stuck in its holder on the top of an IBM Selectric computer recorder.

Before her were two consoles of buttons. One transmitted and one received. The transmitter was composed of 12 square buttons, ten with numbers and letters, and two with signs. Each gave off a different musical note as you touched them. With practice, you could play the *William Tell Overture* on it.

The receiver was composed of several flat disks and a computer display screen tinged in green. The flat disks across the bottom read STOP, PLAY, RECORD, REWIND, FAST FORWARD, LOCK, and HOLD. The display screen flashed READY in the upper left-hand corner. A small switch was nicked to ON.

Viki sat in a small room off the cafeteria in the computer section of Yale's Hancock College. She was wearing a red turtleneck sweater and green corduroys. She cracked her knuckles and pressed the RECORD and PLAY buttons on the Honeywell.

The READY flashed off the screen and RECORDING took its place.

Viki moved over to the IBM and punched out a seven-digit number to the tune of *Twinkle, Twinkle, Little Star.* Viki's left hand stabbed the LOCK and HOLD buttons on the Honeywell and waited.

The IBM clicked several times as the preprogramming code took effect. The receiving code located the sending computer's code, digested it, edited it, reshuffled it, organized it, and pinpointed it.

A 914 appeared in the center of the green Honeywell screen. Shortly thereafter a RYE, NEW YORK AND VICINITY appeared under the 914 area code.

Viki leaned over and switched the IBM to OFF. She then programmed a retrieval and eraser code into the Honeywell. She stood up and went to dinner.

She ordered a cold roast-beef sandwich on rye with both mustard and ketchup while thinking about the man Chiun called "Emperor." He was from Rye, New York.

Viki thought about her father's death and Remo and Chiun. Then she went home and packed her things.

Remo answered the door. Chiun was sitting in the center of their Fairfield, Connecticut, motel room fiddling with the parchment daytime drama as if nothing had happened that night.

Remo was waiting for room service to bring up some rice when the knock had come. There was no reason not to think that it was room service, since Remo had called 45 minutes ago and the kitchen always seemed to get the order wrong.

Either they cooked the rice with artificially preserved meat or they topped it with a sauce packed with monosodium glutamate or any number of other things that were poison to his system.

But now there was no smell of food or sound of wheels on a rolling cart so Remo opened the door with his left hand, holding his cut hand behind him.

Viki Angus leaped into the room and threw her arms around him.

"Remo, Remo. Thank God," she cried, crushing her ample bosom, hardly held back behind her braless chambray shirt, upon him. She sank her head onto his shoulder and wracked the room with sobs.

Chiun watched, then began to scribble furiously on his parchment.

"Easy now," Remo said, moving Viki over to the bed and sitting her down. "What happened?"

Viki cried into her hands a bit more, then looked up toward the door.

"I was home alone. And I was so frightened, and then I looked out the window and I thought I saw, I thought I saw... it was awful." She leaped up and grabbed Remo again. "I don't even want to think about it."

"Easy," Remo repeated as she squirmed across his body again, rubbing her thigh across his front. "What was it? You've got to tell us if you want us to help."

"Don't leave me," Viki sobbed. "Don't ever leave me." Her breasts bombarded his chest again.

"Don't worry. You're all right now. Calm down and I'll get you some water."

Viki's wracking sobs began to subside. "All right," she said meekly. She watched as Remo went into the bathroom and water began to run.

Then she noticed Chiun at her side. She hastily frowned again, trying to bring on more tears.

"When you entered," Chiun said, "did you say 'Remo, Remo, thank heavens' or 'Remo, Remo, thank God?'"

Viki looked at him, trying for vulnerability, and said, "Thank God, I think."

"Thank you," said Chiun, scratching something out on his parchment and then writing something else.

Remo came out with a glass of water and sat on the bed next to Viki.

She sipped slowly.

"Now this thing in the yard," Remo said. "What was it? You saw people?"

"That's right, Remo. People. People. In my yard."

"Many of them? Were they Orientals? How many? Three? Four?"

"Four, I think. But it was dark. And they looked like Orientals, I'm pretty sure. Oh, it was awful."

Remo looked toward Chiun. "Looks like they're after Viki too," he said.

Chiun shrugged.

"We'll have to bring her to Houston with us."

Chiun shrugged again.

There was a knock on the door.

Viki screamed. Remo looked toward the door. Chiun continued writing.

"Room service," came a hesitant voice from outside.

"Tell them to take back the rice," said Chiun without looking up. "I smell gravy."

CHAPTER SEVEN

THE LEADER CALMLY EXPLAINED what they had to do.

The leader calmly explained that the attack had not failed, it had succeeded.

The leader coughed three times, hacked once, and spit a hunk of phlegm into the garbage can of the eighteenth-floor suite of the Houston, Texas, Sheraton.

"But we lost three of our best men," said a voice in Chinese.

"We have gained knowledge," was the leader's reply. "We have gained understanding." The leader weighed the two in his mind. "It is regrettable," he said at last. "But it was necessary. Tell me, what have we learned?"

The young Chinese voice told the old man about the attack at Meatamation and how the white man leveled three of the Creed's best fighters. Then the voice spoke of the yellow man who had been waiting outside Meatamation.

"The yellow man," whispered the leader, raising his right hand toward his eye. His right forefinger stopped at his left breast but his eight-inch fingernail rested just below his left eye. "Were his eyes the color of steel?"

"Yes," was the answer.

"It is as I feared," said the leader. "He has come. He has finally come." The leader dropped his hand to his lap and bent his head in silent prayer. He remained that way for a minute and a half, then his ancient head rose.

"Have you paid the others?"

"The marchers? Yes."

"Do they know of our creed?"

"No."

"Have you replenished our ranks?"

"Hired some new men? Yes."

"Call the others," said the leader. "The time approaches. We must do it. Now."

After the young person had left the room, the leader raised himself from his chair. His rise was slow as were his movements and speech. He finally got to his standing height of four feet eleven, then shuffled across the nylon-pile hotel carpet to the drawn curtains.

A shaking left hand gripped the heavy green material and wrenched it open. Hard, hot sunlight poured over the leader into the room. Houston hung in space, shiny gray, as if some hand had smeared Vaseline over it.

Big cars, each looking newly painted, jockeyed with the dirty, tan hulks of the tractor trailer trucks for 10 clear yards of road space. Work crews were pulling off the red-and-green decorations from the streets, heralding the passing of the new year. Stores were ending their post-Christmas sales.

And it was hot in Texas. It was always hot. That's why the leader liked it here better than Connecticut. It was hot. That was all the leader cared about. That was all he felt. That was all he saw.

Because the leader's eyes were bright blue, but the pupils were dark, smoky white. The leader was completely blind.

He heard the door open. The others had returned.

"Sit down, please," said the leader in Chinese.

"Sit down," said another, translating in English.

The leader waited until he heard two bodies settle into the suite's chairs, then he closed the curtain, and shuffled back to his chair, secure in the knowledge that no outstretched leg or upright body would obstruct his path.

The leader lowered himself into his blood-red seat with the green fanged dragons carved from wood resting beneath his arms.

"Sinanju is here," he said. "Lo, after many millennia, we cross paths finally."

"We have to kill a few more people," was the translation.

"We will not attack," continued the leader. "Our history tells of many dead men who tried to attack the steel-eyed Koreans. And now he is doubly dangerous because of the white man with tiger's blood."

"We will not attack," was the translation.

"We will separate and destroy," said the leader.

"We will separate and destroy," said the translator.

The other body in the room shifted and said: "Same difference."

The leader asked for a translation. He was asked, in Chinese, "Many pardons, wise one. But is that not the same thing as a two-sided attack?"

"Idiot," the leader flared. "You can bang your head against a wall all day and it will not come down. But pull out the right brick and it will collapse in ruin."

"Naw," was the translation. "It's not the same thing."

The leader heard another shuffle of cloth against leather. A voice said, "Do we have to kill them in the same manner as before? The new men can't understand why we have to skin them and put them in trees."

There was a translation.

"Fools, fools, fools," said the leader. "It is tradition. It is legend. It is our strength. For not only do we achieve death in our victims but fear in their survivors."

The leader's right temple was throbbing. "We are the last of my kind. The black plague, it was us. The famine of 1904, it was us. And now, now we are about to embark on the great prophesy of my creed. The road must be kept pure for our followers."

"The old man says keep doing it," said the translator.

"That is all," said the leader, waving his hand. "Now, listen, and take this down."

The translator pulled out a pad and pencil and wrote what the leader said for the next 10 minutes.

"Prepare your people," said the leader.

"Let's go," said the translator.

The leader listened as two bodies moved slowly away, a door opened, then closed.

The leader slumped down in his seat. The years, the strain had weakened him. He could not let them see it, but it had. His followers now had to be paid to take up the Creed. They no longer spoke the mother tongue. They could no longer change into other shapes or take on other forms. He was the last. Only he.

His forces had shattered. This was his last chance. All that was left to follow was the legend. The legend of the Final Death.

The leader moved slowly across the room to the bed. He eased his old and frail body down. He stared, unseeing, up to the plaster ceiling. His mind clouded and he was back. Back with his kind in Ti-Ping village.

He remembered the rooms of gold, paid in tribute to the cult's power and the cult's God. The only true God, the ruler of the realm of the afterlife.

He remembered his leader, his true father, telling him, teaching him the lesson of the Final Death.

The leader lay on his gold and blue Sheraton bed cover in the warm Houston afternoon and mouthed the words as he remembered.

The stomach is the center. The house of all life and death. Life begins and ends there. The soul dwells there. Destroy the stomach and destroy all life. When you die, you die the Final Death.

No place in the afterlife. No place by God's side. We are the holy saviors of the stomach. We wander the earth as the undead, slaves to our God, punishers of all transgressors.

The leader remembered the deaths.

The cutting off of all lifeblood. The slitting of the throat.

The release of the life force. The slicing down to the stomach.

The destruction of the Holy House. The stripping of the carcass.

The homage to our God. The skeleton in the tree, symbolizing our strength and power.

The Final Death. The burial of the innards.

Thus it had been for thousands of years. Before the cult moved out of China and up into Rumania, Russia, Lithuania, Transylvania, their legend had grown enormously. Tales of their ability to change into trees and nebulous forms ran amok through the villages.

But the power had shifted outside mother China. The deaths continued, the creed grew, but the legend was lost. The white men saw them as farcical bloodsuckers. Men of swarthy complexion and burning eyes. They were remembered as hissing, caped servants of the Devil, napping into bedrooms and sinking their teeth into the breasts of fleshy women.

The deaths continued but the true purpose was lost. Their ranks dwindled as, one by one, the leader's companions were released. They had done their work well and so, they entered the afterlife.

Until there was no one left but him. He had moved and planned and killed but it was not enough. His God wanted more. So he moved to America, the center of meat-eating, stomach-destroying madness. He had taken the age old secrets of the cult and planned the final, massive destruction of transgressors.

But times had changed. He had grown old and weak and the blindness was sent down as punishment. So now he used the rooms of gold for pay. And now he gave the age old secrets to outsiders for implementation.

The gold was beginning to run low, but the plan was near completion. Soon his God would be satisfied. Soon he would be released to join his companions.

But first they had to deal with Sinanju. First they had to send the white man and the Korean to their Final Deaths. There had been a truce centuries ago but it was ended.

CHAPTER EIGHT

"Why are you wearing that ridiculous costume?"

Viki Angus looked down at her blue mini-length dress with the gold braid on the sleeve, then back at Remo. "What's ridiculous? This is an official Star Trek lieutenant's uniform. I always wear it when I'm flying."

"You're not one of them, are you?" Remo asked.

"One of who?"

"One of those Starkies," Remo said.

"Trekkies," Viki corrected. "And I'd rather not be called that. Now, quiet while I get this ship into a holding orbit."

She pressed her lunch tray several times, making bleeping noises.

Across the aisle, a manufacturer of toilet seats looked up at the noise.

"Landing coordinates locked in," Viki said.

The overhead loudspeaker beeped, and the stewardess' voice insinuated out: "Please fasten your seat belts. We will be landing momentarily in Houston."

Viki uncrossed her legs and fastened her safety belt, pulling up her dress another inch. The toilet-seat manufacturer lowered his magazine to watch more carefully.

A few minutes later, the plane slapped onto the runway and moved toward the unloading docks. The loudspeaker hoped they had all enjoyed their flight.

Viki bounced up in her seat and commended loudly the spaceship's navigational officer. The toilet-seat manufacturer rose slowly, mopping his brow.

"How come the gorgeous ones are always nuts?" he muttered to no one in particular.

Viki, oblivious, reached up over her seat to get her bag, the one with *The United Federation of Planets* stenciled in silver under a blue-and-silver insignia comprised of two silhouettes surrounding a star system.

The male population of first class moved their heads in unison to chart the rise of Viki's hemline with the rise of her arm. A small disappointed sip of breath came when an Oriental in a flowing green kimono moved behind her, blocking the view.

Remo, Chiun, and Viki moved toward the door of the plane where a stewardess invited them to come again.

"Thank you," said Viki. "I'll beam down to the planet now."

The thin, small-chested stewardess watched Viki's exit as she hopped down the stairs, making a bubbling sound. Chiun followed her.

"Are those two together?" the stewardess asked the next man.

"Yes," said Remo, the next man. "That's Captain Jerk and Mister Schmuck."

"It figures," said the stewardess.

Remo, Chiun, and Viki rode the commuter bus to town. They sat across from a fat white woman holding a child to her bosom and Delaware Torrington Junior, known to his contemporaries as D.T. 2.

D.T. 2 held a radio tape deck close to his ear. It was playing a new rock number at a decibel level that would have succeeded in banning the Concorde jet from the entire civilized world.

Delaware Torrington Junior slumped down in his seat so he could look up Viki's dress. "Oooooh, mama," he groaned aloud.

Viki caught his stare, pushed her knees tightly together, and sat closer to Remo. Remo was thinking about his seat. His feet were pressed against the bottom of his shoes. He moved his body off the bus seat as the driver came onto the bus and started the engine.

Remo slowed his breathing, then lifted his feet off the floor. He pressed back hard against the seat, hard enough to cause a friction that held him in place, three inches over the seat.

Chiun nodded as the bus started. Then Remo slowly released his breath and settled his body weight back onto the seat. No one but Chiun had noticed Remo do his exercise for the day.

Viki pressed his arm. "That person is staring at me," she said.

"Zap him with your phaser," Remo said.

Delaware Torrington Junior rubbed his cap on his lap and leered at Viki while the screeching trumpets on the tape player woke the fat woman's sleeping child. The baby began to cry.

D.T. 2 motioned to Viki and smiled. Remo rose off his seat and leaned forward.

"What do you want?" he said.

"I don't want you," said D.T. 2, loudly over the crashing bongos throbbing against his head. "I want her."

"I'm sorry, sir," said Remo. "Her heart belongs to Star Fleet Command."

"I never heard of that group," said D.T. 2. "Whadda they play?"

"Nothing that would interest you," said Remo. "Music mostly."

"Don't give me no jive, Clive," said Delaware Torrington Junior. He smacked his sneakers on the floor and hissed hysterically at his own wit.

The baby next to him howled even louder as the saxophones on the tape reached a climax. The fat woman asked D.T. 2 if he could turn down the music a bit.

"I can't hear it if I turns it down, fatty," said Torrington.

"Then let's turn it up," said Remo. "So you can hear it really well."

Remo's arm moved out and pressed against the machine at the black man's head. Suddenly the woofer made way for an ear and the tweeter was displaced by a pimpled jaw line. Tubes and transistors were cracked, pushed aside and smashed out the other side of the tape player to make room for an Afro passing through. The back of the bus was suddenly silent except for the tinkling of glass in the aisle.

Remo pulled the bus cord and the driver stopped at the next corner to let off a man with a radio between his ears. Delaware Torrington Junior later would marvel with all his friends about how the tape player retained a perfect outline of his head, even after it was pried loose. The whole experience really shook him. It was a week before he stole another tape player.

The thankful fat woman soothed her child, looked apologetically at Remo and said, "Houston isn't what it used to be."

"Nothing is," said Remo.

"How did you do that?" asked Viki when Remo sat down again. She asked him when they got off the bus, when they registered at the Houston Hilton, and when Remo showed her to her adjoining room. "How did you do that?"

"Find me a radio and I'll show you," said Remo, turning to go.

"Don't you want to come in?" asked Viki seductively.

Remo looked at her, put his hand on his chin, thought for a few seconds, then said, "No."

"Remo," said Chiun from the doorway of the other room. "Come in. We must speak of your soul."

"Yes," said Remo to Viki, not wanting to hear any more fairy tales about his inner being sneaking out to lunch when he had his right hand cut.

"I knew I'd finally get to you," Viki said with a smile.

"Whatever you say," said Remo.

Viki left the doorway of the room and moved over to the single bed. She plopped down on the bed, lifted her uniform hem and smoothed her right nylon from the top of her boot all the way up to her crotch. Then she repeated the procedure on her left leg. Then she took off her black boots, slowly, caressing the leather, filling the room with long, cracking creaks. She repeated the smoothing of her panty hose, from the bottom tippy toe to the very tippy top of her thigh.

Remo leaned against the desk in the room and watched her as if she were a mechanic changing a tire.

"Aaah, that's better," said Viki, stretching her arms above her head, lifting her hem even higher. "Come on. Sit by me and tell me all about yourself."

"Aah, shucks," said Remo. "Not much to tell." He moved toward the bed and Viki grabbed his wrist and pulled him down onto her lap.

"Are we going to meet your friend here?" she asked.

"What friend?"

"The one Chiun calls emperor."

"No. He doesn't get around much," said Remo.

"That's too bad. He seemed nice."

"Sure, he's nice," said Remo. "So are paper clips and pencil sharpeners." Remo slid off her thighs and bounced to a sitting position on the edge of the bed.

"Who do you think killed your father?" asked Remo.

Viki's face closed like an off off Broadway show. But only for a moment. Then her eyes narrowed and she licked her lips.

"Aaah," she breathed more than said, and pulled herself up onto her knees.

"That's no answer," Remo said.

"An interesting question," said Viki, putting both hands again his chest and pushing. "How should I know?"

Remo's body did not move but his hand snaked its way between her knees. "There must have been a reason," he said.

"I don't know wha..." said Viki, arching her back, her head snapping toward the ceiling as Remo's hand moved.

"Didn't your mother or father ever tell you anything that might have given you a clue?" Remo slid off her panty hose and pressed her down onto the pillow.

"No... No. No... nothing," said Viki.

"Anything. Any clue," Remo pressed, moving atop her.

Viki shook her head.

Remo brought her to a galactic interstellar climax with a soft graceful movement of his body. And then to another one and another one, then moved away from her.

"Whooooosh," said Viki. "Way, way, way, way out." She wiped tears from her cheeks and sweat from her brow, then straightened her dress. She stood up and made a sign toward Remo with her left hand, opening a gap between her third and fourth fingers.

"That's a Vulcan salute," she said. "Live long and prosper."

Remo held up the three middle fingers of his right hand. "Boy Scout salute. Be prepared," he said.

He turned toward the door.

"Remo?"

"Yeah?" He turned back.

"How well do you know Chiun?"

Remo watched as Viki pulled a soft, floor-length green bathrobe out of her bag and wrapped it around her.

"Well enough. Why?"

"Well, he told me a little about what he does."

Remo laughed. "You mean write soap operas, belittle white people and moon over hook-nosed singers?"

"No. He talked about killing. You ought to be careful, Remo." Remo blinked. "I'm afraid of him, Remo. I think he might be planning something behind your back."

Remo shook his head and left.

Viki smiled. So the man called "the emperor" wouldn't be here in Houston. It didn't matter. She would kill Remo and Chiun first. And then get the third man.

Charlie Ko waited until the undead settled into his hotel room. Charlie drank a vodka and orange juice from a plastic glass while waiting, careful to keep his right forefingernail away from his face.

Charlie Ko was a born leader of men. He had known it when he was a kid, leading the children of P.S. 189 in New York in unattendance. He knew it as a teenager, when he led the Devil Dragons through seven rumbles in three years to be the number one street gang in Chinatown. And he knew it as a young man, when he moved up to mobilizing student troops at the Chicago Democratic convention.

Charlie had become a master of his craft. All over the east coast, men knew that if you wanted a head busted you came to Charlie Ko.

But it was a long time since those carefree college days when he did it for free. A man with the most skulls on the inside of his locker, signifying acknowledged kills during riots and street fights, just couldn't continue in his magnanimous murderous ways. He had to industrialize, internalize, and incorporate.

So Charlie partnered up with his three best friends from the Chinatown days and went out for hire. Their strike-busting led to body-guarding. Their body-guarding led to clandestine operations. Their clandestine operations led to mercenary mobilization.

And mercenary mobilization led to inquiries by appointment and inquiries by appointment led to his office on Lexington Avenue in New York and his office led to his reputation as the best and that led him to the Houston Sheraton and a final meeting with the undead.

For Charlie's three partners had met their untimely ends in a meat factory in Westport, Connecticut. Up until that time, they had been his arms and legs. They were the ones who had to go flying all over the country to locate and report on possible victims. They were the ones who had to do in those victims. And they were the ones who had to make it look like swine-flu vaccine reactions.

But no more. Charlie was left to complete the leader's instructions with a bunch of raw recruits. Raw, inexperienced, but bloodthirsty recruits.

"Alright," said Charlie, putting the cold plastic glass down and wiping a bit of liquid from his thick, soft lower lip. "Let's get started."

Yat-Sen, Sheng Wa, Eddie Cantlie, Gluck, and Steinberg leaned back in their seats, on the sofa, and on the bed.

Charlie walked to the writing desk and picked up some Sheraton stationery. He handed out the sheets, then moved back to his drink.

"This is our next plan of attack," he said.

A low groan rose from the group. "Another one?" said Eddie Cantlie, who had been in it from the beginning. "That's the fourth one this month."

Charlie shrugged. "Either you control the situation or it controls you."

While the group was checking over the material, Charlie checked over his fingernail. He and his three partners had been outfitted with one of these things when they took the job.

The crazy things I have to do for my art, Charlie thought. Spend every morning varnishing and sharpening the permanently affixed, artificial fingernail blade until it shone like steel and could cut paper.

Three times a day drinking a mixture of vitamins and gelatin to fortify his own nails. Every afternoon spent checking his speed and accuracy until he could pinion olives hurled into the air.

But it was worth it. What he was getting paid for this job would keep his wife, his mistress, his lawyer, his agent, his office, his staff, and his car for two years. If everything went smoothly, and why shouldn't it? He was in charge. If everything went smoothly he had an "option" for continued service at a very pretty price indeed — a share of the combined wealth of the United States of America.

Charlie ran his wet tongue across his full lips. It was his childhood dream come true. He had sat in that mesh enclosed detention room at P.S. 189 waiting for that faggot sadist who passed for an assistant principal to come in, coo appreciatively at him, then slam his fingers in a desk drawer or slam his rear end with a heavy plastic ruler, and Charlie thought about someday being as big as King-Kong, as mighty as Godzilla, and laying the whole country to waste.

The vice-principal had gotten what he deserved when his throat had been cut on the way to dinner at a Chinatown restaurant one night, but the country had yet to pay.

It would. And soon.

"What's this? What's this?"

Sheng Wa was looking up at Charlie, stabbing the sheet of paper near the bottom.

Charlie moved over to the bar and jabbed an orange slice and a cherry with his fingernail. He lifted the fruit shish-kebob and dunked it in his glass.

"What's what?"

"This, at the bottom. We have to kill two more guys?"

"Sure. Separate and destroy. Like it says. Like we did to that guy and his wife."

Yat-Sen spoke up in his thick, careful Oriental accent. "Must we kill them in the same way?"

"That's the way the leader wants it," said Charlie.

"Can't we shoot them?"

"Nope."

"Blow them up?"

"Uh-uh."

"Run them over?"

"No. What's the big deal? It's just two more guys."

"But it's so disgusting," said Yat-Sen, who had been the one holding onto Mrs. Angus' chin, and doing all the giggling.

Now several people in the room laughed.

Charlie looked around. "Shit," he said. "I do all the work. What the hell are you complaining about? I'm the one who sticks the finger in. Look, you get your pay, right?"

Yat-Sen nodded.

"It's enough to keep you and your teenage whores happy, right?"

The group giggled. Yat-Sen turned to them, then smiled.

"I let you wear rubber gloves to strip the carcasses, right?" said Charlie.

"Sure," said Yat-Sen. "But next time, do you have to go through all that Christianity, meat-eating mumbo jumbo?"

Charlie moved directly in front of Yat-Sen and put his fingernail on the bridge of the man's nose.

"If I hear any more of your garbage, Jap, I'm going to pluck out your eyes and make you eat them."

The group howled. Yat-Sen only swallowed and nodded.

Steinberg spoke up. "Same as before?" He was one of the new boys contracted on a rush basis. He had only heard about the butchering of the bodies, but he looked forward to trying it.

"Yeah," said Charlie. "We wait until we get them alone. Then we stick it to them." He stabbed the air with his fingernail.

"You do that," said a voice at the door, "and there won't be enough left of any of you to find."

The group turned toward the sound of the voice. It was the same voice that had told them to finish off a drunken widow in a cellar of Woodbridge. It was the same voice that instructed Charlie's partners to wait at a factory office in Westport for a tall, thin, dark-haired man. And it was the same voice that told them what the old man had to say.

The voice belonged to the leader's top agent in the field, the translator.

The translator walked into the room.

"You know what that man did at Meatamation," said the translator. "By the time you got your fingernail up, your head would be in your hand."

"My partners ain't me, baby," said Charlie Ko.

"You'll wind up like them if you try messing with these characters," said the translator, moving over to the couch and sitting down next to Gluck.

Charlie licked his lips again. "What do you want from me? You heard what the leader said."

"The leader is old. He's senile. He says that this other chink will just stand there and let us slit his throat. Then he thinks that the white guy will be so broken up about it that we'll be able to do anything we want. He's crazy. I've seen these guys. They ain't that bad or that stupid."

"So?" said Charlie Ko.

"So I'll tell the old man that we did as he asked. Then we make sure these guys get it."

"If they're so good, how are we going to do that?"

"I've checked with their room service in Connecticut and here. All they ever order is duck or fish with rice."

Charlie Ko leaned against the bathroom door and smiled.

Eddie Cantlie nodded and pulled out a small rubber stamp with a purple *USDA* on the bottom. He lightly popped it against his hand a couple of times.

The rest of the group looked at the translator like cancer cells waiting to be formed.

"Yeah," said Marion Beriberi Greenscab, the translator. "The fucker lied to me. He ain't no vegetarian."

CHAPTER NINE

TEXAS SOLLY NEARLY LOST HIS LUNCH of gefilte fish and ribs when Remo brought in Jacob and Irving. One over each arm.

Remo dropped them on either side of Texas Solly's big oak desk with the metal legs as Texas Solly started choking and hiccuping at the same time while trying to get on his knees.

Texas Solly's office was half a city away from his slaughterhouse but the smell of death still seemed to hang in the air. Solly's office was a modern, artificially paneled wood affair with aluminum chairs that were guaranteed impossible to get comfortable in.

Irving Pennsylvania Fuller was living up to that guarantee when Remo had padded in. Irving rose quickly, partly from his professional training and partly because it was such a pleasure to get up, and placed his chest on Remo's nose.

"You got an appointment?" asked Irving, flexing his shoulder muscles and pressing the outline of the Smith and Wesson in his shoulder holster against his jacket.

"Have," said Remo.

"What?" Irving said threateningly, since he always said "what" threateningly whenever he was answered by anything but "yes" or "no."

"Have. The question should be 'do you have an appointment?'" said the thick-wristed man in Irving's chest.

"I don't need an appointment," said Irving. "I work here."

Remo had smiled benignly, raised his shoulders, as if to shrug, and Irving felt his middle freezing. He felt a soft pressure on both his hips and then the cold had risen to his head directly along his back and he felt nothing else until he woke up across Texas Solly's desk set.

Remo had taken Irving by the back of the collar and walked through the door marked "Weinstein's Meat and Poultry Sales," until Jacob had run up and thrust his gun out.

"Hey," said Jacob Schonberger. "You can't come in here."

"I just did," said Remo, not wanting to get into the philosophy of being. If Jacob had been as intelligent as Irving was, they could have been in the hall all day discussing the viability of Remo's existence within it.

Jacob had suddenly seen Irving sitting against the back of Remo's leg. He moved back.

"What is this?" he said.

"This is a hallway," said Remo. "I thought we had already established that."

"Did you drop Irving? Jesus, you dropped Irving!" was Jacob's incisive reply. Jacob was a few inches shorter than Irving, but wider. He moved back even farther and thrust his gun out in a straight line toward Remo's chest.

Remo decided against informing him that the uniformly accepted way of pointing a gun at someone was from the hip so that you could not be disarmed if someone just reached out and took off your hand.

But the man looked too agitated to be interested in Justice Department training at that moment.

"What's your name, buddy?" Jacob had asked since his habit was to intimidate his victims by asking them for their names, then telling them, "Alright, so and so, move!" And if he got some wise crack from some mealy mouthed punk, he'd crack the barrel of his .38 between the kid's teeth. It had worked since his days at the correctional facility and had been a comfort to him ever since.

"I'm the man from Hebrew National," said Remo.

Jacob moved by instinct to slash his gun barrel across Remo's face but Remo's face was not where it had been a moment before and somehow Jacob felt his arm swing farther than it had ever swung before.

Then there was a crack and Jacob felt the cold steel of his own gun bouncing off his own face and then he didn't feel anything and wouldn't until he woke, in excruciating pain, in a Houston emergency room three hours later.

There he would wait 45 minutes, rocking to and fro on a wooden bench watching small drops of blood gather in his lap, until a nurse came over to inform him that he would need at least a thousand dollars worth of surgery and did he know his Blue Cross/Blue Shield number?

Texas Solly was trying not to upchuck while kissing Remo's hush puppies. He hacked once more to loosen an acid-tasting piece of fried rib stuck in the back of his throat, swallowed, then begged: "Please, don't kill me yet, let me explain."

Remo looked down critically and slowly pointed at Solly's face.

"You... have some sauce on your cheek," he said. He reached over and pulled a soiled tissue from Weinstein's desk between Irving, who was snoring, and Jacob, whose blood was bubbling between his mashed teeth.

"Thank you," said Texas Solly, wiping his mouth. "You'll let me explain?"

"Go ahead," said Remo.

"These guys weren't for you," Texas Solly began hurriedly, picking himself off his knees and waving at the hulks on his desk. "I was being bugged by an antimeat group recently and..."

"Wait a minute," said Remo. "Was this a bunch of twits waving signs and screaming about swine flu? A redhead in charge?"

"Yeah, that's them," said Solly. "Were they your spies?"

"Never mind," said Remo. "Go ahead with your story."

"Yeah, well," said Solly. "I swore I'd have your shipment or your money today and I'm as good as my word. You can tell Jaccalini that he'll get his steaks and his money back too. You tell Jaccalini that's the stuff Texas Solly Weinstein is made of."

"That's terrific," said Remo, wondering if there could be two Texas Solly Weinsteins in Houston and if he had met the second one. "Where can I find him?"

"Who?" said Solly.

"Jaccalini," said Remo.

Texas Solly stared at Remo for a second. Then he laughed.

WARREN MURPHY & RICHARD SAPIR

"Very funny, Rico. Very funny. You are Rico Shapiro, aren't you?"

Remo shook his head. "Never heard of him," he said.

Texas Solly's laugh took on a brittle quality and his smile grew lopsided. He slowly moved behind his desk, putting his hand under the top drawer, as if for support.

Remo moved over and pushed the alarm mechanism into the floor by pressing his palm through the top of the desk. Texas Solly felt the alarm system brush by his crooked finger.

He swallowed very slowly, looking from the palm-shaped hole in his desk to Remo's face.

"I'm the man from Hebrew National," said Remo. "Talk to me. And no baloney."

Sunset over Sinanju.

"And the colors were the colors of the rainbow. Lo, the pinks and oranges and purples and reds and colors not given names, such was their brilliance, shone across the humble village. Thus had it been, thus shall it always be. Until the ocean meets the sky and the sky meets the earth."

Chiun slowly put down his quill pen and looked over his parchment. Over his shoulder the real sun was really setting over the real Houston.

The purples and oranges here were great heavy coats of carbon monoxide exhaust and factory wastes of all denominations. A solid layer of black contained these vibrant colors and the rest of the sky was bathed in an angry rose.

People in their cars on the highway, in their high-rise apartments and offices were watching this light and thinking it beautiful, not knowing that in fewer years than they cared to think about, perhaps even before they themselves died, these colors would come to claim their children.

These colors would reach beyond all their windows and steel and concrete and air conditioners and humidifiers and slowly choke their sons and their daughters to death.

The death of America would not come with a bang or a whimper. It would come with a gurgle.

Chiun, the Master, thought of this and so brought the sun down across his tiny fishing village, his home, of Sinanju.

Where the people only breathed the smell of fish and the salt of the sea.

There was a tiny knock on the hotel door. Before that, there had been the careful padding of feet across the hall carpet. Then the minute air displacement of a curved, long-haired body outside the door. And then, clearly, the fast incorrect breathing of one trying to control excitement.

Chiun did not let all this racket disturb his work. That was the kind of writer he was.

"Come in, my child," he said. "I am finished now."

The door opened a crack and then there was another tiny knock.

"Chiun? It's me, Viki. Can I come in?"

Without waiting for an answer, she let the door slowly swing open to expose... her.

She stood in the hallway with her long brown hair cascading across her head and shoulders like thick waves of water over a mountainside. Her brown eyes were wide and clear and her soft, full, rose lips were slightly parted.

She was dressed in a floor-length cotton robe which swept in at her waist and under her full breasts which were now crashing against the soft fabric in great heaves.

She stood still for a heartbeat then swung into the room, closing the door behind her.

Chiun remained with his back toward the window in the lotus position. Viki oozed across the room toward him, sinking onto her knees as she grew near.

"I was frightened," she breathed. "All alone in my room..."

She let the sentence die since Chiun seemed grandly disinterested. She instead lowered her body onto the sides of her legs to give the little Oriental a better view of her breasts. Chiun looked across the expanse that was Viki Angus and intoned: "We are never truly alone."

"I know," sighed Viki, more in relief than the comfort of company. "I have you and... and Remo."

"What has he done to deserve two ands?" asked Chiun.

Viki did not like that. She did not like the way the little Oriental seemed to read her mind every time she opened her mouth or made a move. If she were not so sure of herself she could have sworn he was humoring her.

But the little man was human, so a little skin and a few words in his ear would surely get a rise out of him. It had worked on Remo, it should work on Remo's partner.

Viki shifted her position to bring her naked leg up and out from under her cotton robe. The garment fell back, hanging over one creamy naked thigh, which rose in front of two nearly naked creamy breasts, which were just under a creamy naked neck and a painfully innocent creamy naked face.

"How well do you know Remo?" she asked tentatively.

"You see," said Chiun. "As long as the mind questions, seeks answers, investigates new areas of endeavor, we are never truly alone. Often, while pondering many questions of the day, I feel comforted with the memories of my ancestors. No, one is truly never alone."

Viki stared, wondering if perhaps the old man was a diversion, prepared by the Bureau of Agriculture to take the heat off their main agent, Remo.

No matter, Viki thought. They were both involved in the murder of her parents. They both had to die.

Perhaps Chiun went for a more intellectual approach. Viki tucked her leg back under her robe and moved her head in conspiratorially.

"The reason I ask is that I accidentally recorded a top-secret computer transmission at Yale and... well, Remo was named on it."

Chiun turned quickly toward her and said, "Ah, you see. With machines we can derive comfort and pleasure. I have a machine that records my daytime dramas. That is, it did before they failed me. Tell me, is not your computer like my machine?"

Finally, she had gotten a rise out of the old man.

"No, uh, my machine performs calculations."

"It does as you ask it?"

"Well, not everything."

"Is it infallible?"

"In a limited sense."

"Does it think?"

"Well, no, it doesn't think, really."

"No wonder Remo was on it," Chiun said. And then the Master was silent.

Viki jumped to her feet and angrily pointed down at the Korean.

"I was trying to be nice about this, but you leave me no choice. Remo made love to me. What do you think of that?"

Chiun looked up. "Did he do well?"

Viki hugged herself hysterically and flung her head up to the ceiling.

"It was the most magnificent experience of our entire lives!"

Chiun nodded. "Good, he has improved. Tell me, near the finish, did he breathe through his mouth or through his nose? I have always thought nasal control the far superior."

Viki backed toward the suite's door.

"You little Jap. Remo and I are running away. He's leaving you and your Emperor or Smith or whatever. And there's nothing you can do to stop us."

Chiun remained seated. "Just because you are trying to destroy us is no reason to become insulting. Calling me Japanese is demeaning."

But Viki had screamed after the word "insulting" and stormed out. She slammed the door so hard that Chiun felt the vibration of the sound waves even minutes afterwards.

He considered Viki's actions and came to a decision.

"Cute girl," said Chiun aloud, going back to his parchment. "Cute girl."

CHAPTER TEN

"REMO, WHAT IS A COMPUTER?"

Chiun had asked that on the fifth digit of a seven-digit number with the area code of nine one four that changed every two weeks.

That was this year. Last year, during all the trouble, what with the military learning about CURE and the House of Sinanju freelancing a Greek assignment, the number had been changed every day.

Sometimes it connected to an inner sanctum in a sanitarium, sometimes it connected to a desk outside, sometimes the connection was never completed or the line screeched in his ear, but today, Remo got hold of Dr. Harold Smith very easily. He completed the seven-digit number, the line rang eight times and then the citric acid New England voice filled his ear.

"Hello?"

"Smitty, what is a computer?"

"Remo, what is this? Do you have anything to report?"

"Smitty, why do you always answer a question with a question?"

"I don't always."

"You're no fun. What's a computer?"

A lemony sigh floated halfway across the country.

"If I must, I suppose I must. A computer is an electronic automatic machine for performing calculations. Or one who computes."

"Chiun, it's a machine that computes."

"What is to compute?" asked Chiun.

"What is to compute?" asked Remo.

"To determine or calculate by mathematical means," said Smith.

"To calculate by mathematical means," said Remo.

"What is calculate?" asked Chiun.

"What is calculate?" asked Remo.

"To reckon by exercise of practical judgment. Is this important?"

"Not at all," said Remo to Smith. "To reckon by exercise of practical… what was that last word again, Smitty?"

"Judgment," said Smith.

"Judgment," said Remo.

"What does that mean?" asked Chiun.

"Yeah, what does all that mean?" asked Remo.

"Remo, tell Chiun that it is a machine that artificially thinks and if he wants one, I will try to arrange it. Report, please."

"Chiun," said Remo. "It is a machine that plugs in and then thinks."

"Aha," said Chiun. "I thought so. Very wise. You build machines to think for you since you cannot. Who builds these thinking machines? Koreans?"

"Excuse me for a second, Smitty," said Remo into the phone. "No, we do," he told Chiun.

"You who cannot think build machines that can? How do you do this?"

"Pardon me again, Smitty," said Remo into the phone.

"Do you want to call back?" said Smith's tired voice.

"No, it's all right," said Remo. "I called collect."

A screech like teeth biting a blackboard sounded as Remo dropped the phone on the bed.

"The machines are programmed for logic," Remo said to Chiun, then tried to explain the nebulous meaning of programming. "It's built into them."

"A child can learn what he is not taught," said Chiun. "He can learn from the skies, the earth, the sea. A piece of metal cannot."

"They do all right," said Remo, conscious of the phone on the bed and drawing the conversation on. "Already they do most of the *menial*," he stressed menial, "*petty*," he stressed petty, "jobs in this country."

"A child can unlearn lies," Chiun pressed. "He can grow within himself to discover truth. A piece of metal cannot."

"Well, you better get used to the thought of computers. We work for one giant one."

"I am glad we work for this country now," said Chiun. "For in a few years this nation will be unable to move."

The Oriental turned to find his parchment and incorporate the line about what a child can learn.

Remo went back to the phone.

"Hello, Smitty?"

The answer was a dial tone.

Remo called again and this time the line rang 16 times.

"Are you finished?" asked Smith when he lifted the receiver.

"Sure," said Remo.

"Report," said Smith.

"Friendly little devil, aren't you?" said Remo.

"Haven't you had enough fun with me today?" asked Smith.

"I can never have enough fun with you," said Remo.

Smith sighed again. "I suppose if you were ever nice to me, I'd worry. Report."

"You should have let me lean on the Government swine flu program. I've hit a dead end here."

"Why?"

"Well, Angus led to Peter Matthew O'Donnell. That's two L's on O'Donnell. He wound up in the same place as Mr. and Mrs. Angus. That's one S on Angus."

"So I heard. Go on."

"O'Donnell led to Texas Solly Weinstein. And that's where the trail ends."

"Is he dead, too?"

"No."

"Has he disappeared?"

"No."

"You couldn't make him talk?" Smith's voice took on an edge of incredulity.

"No. I mean yes. I made him talk."

"Then what's the trouble?"

"The trouble is that he didn't know anything. Lots of times and places but no names or faces."

"Go on."

"Texas Solly is up to his neck in hundreds of deals. He's informing the Mafia on the CIA. He's informing the CIA on the Mafia. He's informing the police on the FBI and vice-versa. He's reporting on and to the Board of Health, the Department of Integration, the Bureau of Immigration, and the PTA. The guy's got so much action that somebody in Texas burps and half the free world knows about it. The guys doing the poison and people-peeling are just another phone number and $5,000 to him."

"Are you sure?"

"What do mean, 'Are you sure?' Sure I'm sure. Ask him yourself. Call up Houston information and ask for the General Hospital. He might not be able to speak so well now, but a nurse can get him a pencil, then translate."

"I've never doubted your methods, Remo. And I understand. He was reporting to us as well."

"To CURE? You must be the one he called the cheapskate."

"We paid him $200 a report," Smith said.

"Yeah, you're the cheapskate all right."

"You're entitled to your opinions. Anyway, I have some news."

"Which is?" said Remo.

"The scientists we've had working on this poison. They report that even without the swine-flu shots, the poison becomes inactive after awhile."

"What does that mean?"

"As best we can determine, that means the poison is harmless. Whoever put the poison into the meat system has waited too long. It's too late."

"You mean it's over? That's it?" asked Remo.

"No. There are still some crazy people sticking skeletons in trees and some people who wanted to poison the whole country. I'd still like us to do something about them."

"Make work," said Remo. "Always make work."

In the Hilton Hotel kitchen, a sallow man was preparing a duck in the walk-in freezer, while hopping back and forth from one foot to the other.

The duck had been killed, and was being gutted, plucked, and prepared to the express specifications of a little Oriental on the hotel's 12th floor.

The Oriental had sent back every dish so far that week because it was cooked wrong. Tonight, the Hilton chef vowed to his assistant he would get it right. The customer was always correct. He had sent the new kitchen boy to prepare the fowl for cooking.

The new kitchen boy, who was more of a man and had begun work that day, and would, strangely, never be seen again by the Hilton service staff, now plucked the duck, emptied it of its gizzards, split it, cut it into portions, then took out a small rubber stamp and a thin pad sealed with wax. The wax was indented with the face of a fanged dragon.

The new kitchen boy broke the seal and stamped each section of duck with a light blue *USDA* which would come off during cooking.

"That's wonderful news, Smitty. Where does it leave me?"

"I suggest you go back to the Angus's. They were killed for a reason. I'm checking various aspects of Vincent's last report. You should talk with his daughter, Victoria, again."

Smith hung up.

Remo slowly put the phone down. Now where was Viki anyway?

"Chiun, have you seen Viki?"

Chiun was sitting on his mat in the middle of his room with his eyes closed.

"She is in her room," he said slowly. "Plotting our end."

Remo cocked his head at the Korean, then decided not to pursue the subject further. Chiun might decide to start talking about fangs and escaping souls again.

"Well, I'll call for dinner and invite her in."

"Good," said Chiun. "Maybe the kitchen will get the duck right tonight."

Remo knocked on Viki's door and waited until he heard a tearful, "Come in."

He entered and saw her stretched across the bed in her Star Trek uniform, crying into the pillow. When she turned and saw him, she leaped up and ran into his arms.

"Oh, Remo," she cried. "Thank heavens! I heard you come in and you were so long in there with that, that Chiun, and I thought he may have... he may have... oh thank God you're all right!"

She clutched his neck and buried her head on his shoulder. Remo stood holding her quaking body wondering what the hell she thought she was doing. He remembered her doubts before, her veiled innuendos, and Chiun's comment. Plotting their end?

Viki sobbed a few more times in his shoulder. Remo felt like laughing hysterically. The protectee was trying to kill the protectors, thinking they were the people peelers. Say *that* five times fast.

Remo patted her back.

"There, there, it's okay. Don't worry about Chiun. I know what I'm doing. Come on over and eat."

Viki looked up at him with her tear-stained eyes. The sobs stopped and her voice became ominous.

"Well, all right, but be careful. Be very, very careful."

The two moved into Remo's room, Viki a step behind him and moving very, very carefully.

This was it, she thought. If the Oriental hadn't told Remo about this afternoon already, he was surely about to. And then she would be forced to play her hand.

But when Chiun saw her, all he did was smile sweetly and say: "Duck tonight."

Viki ducked quickly.

"No," said Remo. "We're having duck for dinner. We had fish last night, so we're having duck tonight. Only the 213th duck I've had for dinner in the last year. Yummy yum yum."

Viki sat tentatively on the bed and watched Remo dial room service. Chiun sat placidly in the middle of the floor, eyes again shut. Could it be a trap, thought Viki.

Could Chiun have already told Remo and his calling room service be a code to get a team of eliminators up here? If that were the case, she would have to play her hand.

Remo finished talking and sat down on the bed. He patted Viki's knee which made her jump back a half a foot. Remo looked at her strangely, then lay back, putting his feet up on the bed.

They are both relaxing, thought Viki. It must be a ploy to get her to relax too. And when her defenses were down, they would kill her. Remo would take a pillow and suffocate her. Or Chiun would hold her while Remo cut her throat. Or...

Viki suddenly realized that "room service" could be the clean-up detail. The ones who would strip her carcass and put her skeleton up in a tree.

Well, they had another thing coming. Let Remo attack her. She'd play her hand. Her hand was just itching to be played.

It was itching to be played for 50 minutes. It was itching when Remo went to sleep. It was itching when Chiun started to sway and sing softly, filling the room with the sound of a high-pitched buzz saw going through a dead tree. It was itching when there came a knock on the door.

Viki leaped up and screamed. Remo was up and across the room before she had even gathered her breath. He swung open the suite door and the bellboy outside jumped across the hall.

His tray of food rattled as the boy looked at Remo's tight face and rumpled clothing. He looked beyond to where Viki stood in her Star Trek suit biting her lower lip. Great beads of sweat slipped across her neck and down her cleavage. The bellboy looked at the small, swaying form of Chiun sitting on the floor.

"Heh, heh," he said. "I hope I didn't interrupt anything. Heh, heh, heh. This is the room that ordered the duck, right?"

"Right," said Remo.

"Of course," said the bellboy as if it figured. "Boiled with rice as per your instructions."

"Right," said Remo again. "I'll take it in."

"Of course," the bellboy likewise repeated. "Whatever turns you on." He leered toward Viki and winked at Remo.

Remo pulled the cart into the room, pivoted, and with his hip closed the door on the bellboy's outstretched hand.

"Ow," said the bellboy. "Why'd you do that?"

"It's what turns me on," said Remo.

He wheeled the cart over in between the beds, seeing Chiun's eyes open and a massive wet spot across Viki's Federation torso.

"Did you take a shower with your uniform on?" he asked.

Viki slid her hands across her body, realizing for the first time how much she was perspiring.

"Uh, no," she said, smiling nervously. "It, it was very hot in my room." She hoped her hand did not show or else she would have to play it.

"Well, come and get it," said Remo pleasantly. He lifted the cover and, surprisingly, steam rose to the ceiling. In his hotel experiences, the food usually got to the room ice cold. Except for the iced water, of course, which was warm.

"Smells good," said Chiun, rising from his mat as smoothly as the rising steam.

"It smells bland," said Remo.

"Bland in American means good," Chiun instructed Viki. "It is their way of saying I can eat this without boiling my taste buds, curdling my insides, or blocking my passages. Do you want to know what bad means?"

Viki was not buying. She backed up behind the bed and sat down, crossing her legs to bring her hem up.

"Bad means anything that tastes good," said Remo from the other bed, dishing out the duck. "Bad means spicy, bad means fried, bad is Italian, Jewish, French, Mexican, or Chinese cooking."

"Especially Chinese," said Chiun, taking a full plate from Remo's outstretched hand. "See how easy it is to learn when you listen?"

Remo dished up another hearty portion.

"Here," he said to Viki. "You're a growing girl. Eat." He stuck the plate out to her.

This is it, Viki thought. This is their plan. They had gotten their instructions from the Smith guy. They could not get anything from her so now they were going to kill her just like they killed her mother and her father. But they knew she was too big and too smart to attack directly so they were going to poison her.

Yes, that was it. They were going to knock her out with a drug in the food. Then, when she was helpless, they would use her voluptuous body any way they chose and prepare her for her last place in the branches.

This was it. She was ready. This was it. She would have to play her hand. This was it. She was prepared. This was it.

Viki swung her arm, smacking the plate from Remo's hand, the duck spinning onto the floor and the rice spreading through the air like confetti. Remo watched the plate drop to the rug and Chiun caught the falling portion of duck and put it on his dish.

Viki reached up her dress with her other hand, struggled for a moment, then pulled a snub-nosed .38 revolver from between her legs.

"No," she screamed. "You won't get me. Your plan won't work, Mr. Remo Nichols or whoever you are. Your murder spree is coming to an end right here and now."

She stopped yelling because Remo was not listening to her. He was dishing out another plate of food.

"You hear me?" Viki screamed. "You killed my parents and now I am going to kill you."

"Did not," said Remo from the bed.

"You did. Don't deny it. I know all about your Rye spy ring."

Remo looked up. "All right, kill me. Can I eat first?"

Viki felt as if she was going crazy. Her body began to shake and her skin turned cold. She tried very hard to keep her arms steady.

"No. You can't eat first. You did not let my mother eat before you cut her throat and ripped her skin from her bones and put her up in a tree."

"He would not have done that," Chiun spoke up indignantly. "He would have killed her quickly and left her there."

"Thanks for all your help," said Remo.

"It is nothing," said Chiun.

"Shut up. Both of you," Viki wailed hysterically, her hair flapping against her wet cheeks. "I just wanted you to know that I knew. Now you will die."

Remo shrugged. "If we must, we must." Chiun started to eat.

Viki stared at them in horror, as if she were just beginning to realize that the man seated before her was just seconds away from becoming a torn and bloody hunk of meat. That, seconds from now, she would put a bullet through his body that would tear through his skin and rip out his organs. That blood would spurt out, soaking into the carpet. That his sphincters would open all at once, staining his clothes and filling the Lysol-protected room with a nauseating thick smell.

Viki pushed the gun in front of her body with both hands, centering it on Remo's collarbone, and pulled the trigger.

A huge, clapping boom filled the room, then, automatically, as her father had taught her, she swung the gun to the next target. She centered the gun on the tiny Oriental's stomach and again pulled the trigger.

The two booms of air, rushing back down the barrel after the lead projectile, traveling faster than sound, moved out, overlapped. Viki shivered and waited until her eyes cleared.

"She did that very well," said Remo, munching on the duck.

"Yes," Chiun replied, also eating. "She is a very clever girl. Did you notice that when she could not divide us, she decided to kill us together at a time of natural weakness?"

Viki stood rooted to the spot. Her gun stayed out before her as she stared at Remo who was now hunched on the bed's pillow, and Chiun who sat six inches back from where he had been a moment ago.

On the end of the bed the cover had been scarred by an ugly black powder burn. Between Chiun's crossed legs and his plate was a small, smoking hole.

It was not possible, Viki thought. I had them pegged. They could not have gotten out of the way of a bullet fired point blank.

Automatically Viki swung to where Remo was now sitting, centered her sights between his eyes and pulled the trigger twice. Without waiting, she swung back to Chiun, blasted at his chest, then, just to be on the safe side, moved her sights up to where the top of his head should have been. She fired again.

"Her stance is solid, her aim is good, and she holds the gun so it will offer the least bucking," said Remo from the room's writing desk. "But she's holding it out instead of down at the hip. She's the second with that problem, today."

"She is not perfect," said Chiun, still sitting, still eating. "Or else why should she be using a gun? However, she shows great promise."

Viki looked at the back of the bed. Two bullet holes had splintered the wood where Remo's head should have been. Where his head was was at the writing desk, shyly smiling.

Chiun was now back to his original position. The only damage Viki could see was the spider web of cracked glass in the window beyond. But she had little doubt that just behind the Korean was another smoking bullet hole.

Slowly, in an unbelieving daze, Viki backed up. She was ready to bolt, expecting the two to charge her any second.

When they did not, she slowly let the empty gun drop from her fingers, turned, and calmly walked out the door.

Remo turned to Chiun. "I had better go get her."

"Let her be," said Chiun. "She will soon realize that we were with her at the time of her mother's death. She will return. Come, eat the duck. It is less bad than usual."

CHAPTER ELEVEN

VIKI DID NOT RETURN. She did not return for the rest of that night or the rest of that morning or even for the rest of the next afternoon.

Remo trotted around Houston twice but found neither hide nor hair of her. No one else he talked to had seen her either. And how many beautiful brunettes in Star Trek uniforms were there in Houston?

When he returned to the hotel room Chiun was standing with his back to the door, looking out on the city through the bullet-shattered window.

As Remo took off his shoes, Chiun said: "It is truly wondrous what man has wrought in the short time that is his history."

"Is that the first line of your daytime drama?" Remo asked irritably. "Remo Williams, Remo Williams?"

"They have created toys too tall for them," Chiun continued. "Machines that destroy countries for centuries as in the Land of Herod. Living things smaller than one strand of a fly's wing that can kill an entire army as in your laboratories."

"You mean nuclear weapons and germ warfare?"

Chiun turned. "All toys to keep from learning oneself."

"Great, little father. Thank you. History lecture over now?"

"You are upset, my son."

"And you're depressing."

"You did not find the clever girl?"

"No. She may have taken a bus. Though for the life of me, I don't know where she kept her money in that outfit."

"Or perhaps she walked into the desert."

"Yeah. Or maybe she hitched a ride into Mexico."

"Or found a friendly sanctuary."

"Or an unfriendly sanctuary."

"Or is even now returning here."

"No matter," said Remo. "I'll just sic Smitty onto her. If anybody can find her, he can."

Remo went into the bathroom. The phone rang.

Remo came out of the bathroom and answered it, face dripping.

"Hello?"

"If you want to see Victoria Angus again," said a grating voice, "listen carefully."

"Good timing," said Remo. "Who says I want to see her again?"

There was a short pause then the grating voice continued.

"If you care about Victoria Angus, you'll listen."

"Who says I care? She wasn't very nice to me last night."

"Are you going to listen or are we going to kill her?"

"You mean I have a choice?"

"If you don't listen she's a dead girl."

"So I don't have a choice after all," Remo said.

"You come to Texas Solly's Vine Square slaughterhouse in half an hour and we'll talk. Come alone or the broad's dead."

"I wasn't planning to bring a date."

The connection was broken. Remo pressed down the receiver button and touch-toned the number of the Folcroft Sanitarium in Rye, New York. There were another eight rings and Smith answered.

"Hello, Smitty. I just got a call."

"So did I. What was your call about?"

"Probably the poisoners. They have Viki Angus and want me to walk into a trap to save her. What was your call about?"

"We think we traced the source of the poison in the meat," said Smith.

"Oh?"

"Yes. We went over Angus's last report and it's apparent now the toughness of the meat around the USDA stamp was caused by the poison."

Remo whistled. "So all I have to do is wipe out the Department of Agriculture, right?"

"There's a government inspector at every packing plant," Smith said. "It wouldn't be hard to run in a ringer."

"And at slaughterhouses too?" Remo asked.

"Yes. Why?"

"Never mind. I'll be in touch." Remo hung up.

"Little father, I have some business to attend to."

"Remo," said Chiun, unmoving.

"I know, I know. You don't want me to go, right? These vampires will be there and they'll cut my hand again and stick in a straw and suck out my soul like a McDonald's shake, right?"

"No," said Chiun wearily.

"Oh. So you want to come too? You want to help your poor, uneducated pale piece of a pig's ear through his time of crisis?"

"No."

"No?" Remo was surprised. "No?" Remo was amazed, slightly worried and a little bit hurt.

"No," repeated Chiun. "Go with peace, my son. Remember what I have taught you. You are ready. Represent Sinanju."

Chiun turned back to the window. His head was bowed as if in silent prayer. Suddenly he looked small in the big Hilton hotel room and the bright gray mass of Houston stretching beyond.

Remo did not like him looking that way.

"Hey, Little Father. There's nothing to worry about."

And when Chiun did not answer, Remo asked:

"Is there?"

"Nothing, my son," came the small, dead Oriental voice. "It is day, so beware the shimmering mists. When night falls, beware the darkest shadows. Go, my son."

Remo nodded slowly to the old man's back, then moved toward the door. Perhaps Chiun would feel better when Remo got back with Viki.

"Remo."

Remo turned to see Chiun facing him. "I have no doubt of you," Chiun said.

97

Remo nodded. "Don't have any doubts, Little Father. And when I get back, then we'll figure out how we're going to take the television world by storm with your new daytime drama."

"I have no doubt of you," Chiun repeated.

The door closed behind Remo and he drifted down the hall, not hearing Chiun continue speaking to himself.

"But I have doubt of us. It is their secret that they divide to kill. Yet if we do not divide, we run the chance of both dying. Here, if one dies, the other may yet live and learn enough from that dying to wash this evil away from the earth forever. Be careful, my son."

Gluck sat across the street in a second-floor sequin-wholesaler's shop with a closed sign on the outside hall door. A pair of heavy binoculars were stuck on his eyes and a large, dull green canister was between his legs.

"What if he goes out the back way?" asked Yat-Sen.

"Charlie said he'd come out the front way," said Gluck.

"Why are you using those stupid binoculars? You can see the entrance from here," said Yat-Sen.

"Charlie said that we had better not miss him," said Gluck.

"Charlie said, Charlie said," said Yat-Sen in disgust.

Gluck laughed and Yat-Sen joined him.

"Now cut that out," hooted Gluck, still holding the binoculars to his eyes. "We have to make sure we don't miss him."

"What do you mean we, Kimosabe?" said Yat-Sen. "I don't know about you, but I'm going back to that pretty little bookkeeper."

Gluck lowered the field glasses and turned, saying irritably: "I thought I told you to kill her. We can't have any witnesses."

"I will, I will," said Yat-Sen. "But she helps me pass the time. She jumps so high when I touch her *there*." He giggled.

"You killed the other one though, right?" asked Gluck, turning back to the window.

"Sure. He's back there with her now. You want to check?"

"Naw," said Gluck, bringing the binoculars back up to his eyes. "Have fun."

"Sure," repeated Yat-Sen who moved across the wood floor in the wood-paneled sequin supply store. He moved through beautiful multicolored designs strung from the ceiling, hung on the walls, and bags of sequins stacked on the floor until he reached the door for the back room.

Gluck turned quickly when he heard the knob creak and saw the back of a bloody gray head on the floor and a blonde girl strapped to a wooden chair with leather belts and knee socks. Her rose-colored shirt was open to the waist, her denim skirt was pulled up around her hips, and her stockings were rammed deep down her throat.

Gluck heard a dim, muffled sobbing and choking before Yat-Sen closed the door behind him. Gluck shook his head in amazement at what some people found kicky, then went back to his stake-out.

Five minutes later he saw a tall, thin man in a black T-shirt and blue slacks come out the main entrance and talk to the bell captain.

The bell captain replied silently, then pointed west. In the direction of Texas Solly's Vine Square Slaughterhouse. The bell captain began to call up a taxi but the man in the black T-shirt held up his hand and began to lope in a western direction.

Gluck put the binoculars down, stood up, and slowly closed the window.

"That's it," he shouted.

As he moved toward the back room, he heard the faucet running behind the closed door. Then Yat-Sen came out, drying his hands on his pants. Before he closed the door behind him Gluck saw that the chair was empty. He just glimpsed the back of a shapely leg behind the bloody gray head before the door closed.

"Took a fancy to her, did you?" asked Gluck, smiling.

"Naw," said Yat-Sen. "She choked to death before I even started."

"Too bad," said Gluck. "Let's go."

Yat-Sen collected the thin rubber hose while Gluck retrieved the green canister with the spigot on top.

"Do we have to wear the red costumes this time?" whined Yat-Sen, who was disappointed that he had to have sex with a dead girl instead of one who fought and he could beat up.

"Why bother?" said Gluck. "Charlie and Mary don't care anymore.

Who's going to tell them we didn't? Let's just go up there, do it and peel him. I don't want to miss the action at the slaughterhouse."

The two ran, laughing, across the street, ignoring the traffic, and going through the hotel's swinging doors marked, "Please use revolving doors. Emergency use only."

They ignored the bell captain, the bellboys and the rest of the people in the lobby. They walked to the elevators, carrying the green canister and the rubber hose past the registration desk, the information desk, and the reservation desk. The registration man, the information lady, and the reservation couple did not think to question them.

The elevator operator did. "What's that, guys?" he queried.

"For the air conditioning," said Gluck.

"Twelfth floor," said Yat-Sen.

The elevator operator did not question them further.

Chiun sat on his mat in the middle of the 12th-floor hotel room, seeking solace from his ancestors.

His thoughts went back and back and back and back until he was visiting a deep part of his mind where he rarely went. His childhood. The time, the very short time in childhood he had before he took the role of Master from his father.

His father had been tall and strong and handsome and brave. His hazel eyes had been clear until the very day of his departure from this world. His hands and feet and body were faster than had ever been known. Faster than Remo. Faster even than his own son, Chiun.

Chiun remembered the undead. About how the mist had claimed the leader of their village by day and he had run, gibbering and killing indiscriminately until the Master had brought shame and ruin upon himself by mercifully ending the leader's pain.

By this errand of mercy, for no one else had the strength or the will to raise hand against the leader, so was the Master degraded before all the village. For it was written that no Master of Sinanju would ever hurt another from the village. And his father had killed a leader, a man who required death but did not deserve it.

So, humiliated in the eyes of his people, the Master took himself from those eyes, leaving his family who was still of the village, and went off to die in the hills.

Thus it came to pass that Chiun was the new Master.

Chiun remembered and Chiun hurt.

Chiun hurt.

Chiun opened his eyes.

So deep into meditation had he been that he had not attended to the soft padding of four feet to the outside of his door or the small scratching of a rubber tube being pushed under the door or the small creak of a spigot being turned.

But now, before his mind could sort out these impressions, his eyes saw a shimmering white cloud moving across the room at him.

"The mist, the mist," Chiun cried.

He rose to face the demon cloud. His hands were at his sides, his legs were loose and prepared, but there was nothing to kick at, no living matter to slice through.

His face was twisted in fear but Chiun did not retreat or move back from the oncoming death. If this was to be his end, he would face it as a Master.

The cloud came upon him. It hung about his body, wetting his face and seeping in through his pores. The Master stopped his breathing but still the mist clung. The Master pulled his body in around himself for protection but still the mist infiltrated.

The mist coursed through his very being until it reached the Master's stomach and intestines. There it joined with the remnants of the duck he had the night before and became a deadly nerve-shattering poison.

The Master felt his stomach knot. It was as he always suspected. The stomach was the center of all life and death. It would follow that the soul dwelled there.

Chiun felt heat within his skull and numbness creep up his limbs. Moisture escaped his skin throughout his body. It was his soul trying to escape. His stomach knotted more. His hands became fists. His teeth clenched. The pain. The incredible, unbelievable pain. Pain unknown, unexperienced, amazing.

But Chiun did not cry out. He would not run, gibbering and killing, like the leader of his village. He would die here. He would die at peace because he knew that Remo lived. That the undead had claimed his soul instead of his son's.

Chiun bent double and fell to the carpet beneath the cloud. The mist settled around his fallen body, spread, then dissipated.

Chiun lay on the floor, the pain bending his knees, curling his arms. He did not fight it. He let it come. Through his closing eyes he saw the door to the suite slowly open.

"Worked like a charm," said Gluck. "The new condensed mixture really works fast."

"Yeah, well, let's get it over with," said Yat-Sen, pulling on a pair of rubber gloves.

The two moved into the hotel room to finish off the pathetic, cringing old man.

CHAPTER TWELVE

Mary beriberi greenscab did not want him to move. Neither did Charlie Ko, Sheng Wa, Eddie Cantlie, or Steinberg.

They did not want him to move so badly that two of them were aiming Russian assault rifles at him while a third held an Israeli Uzi submachine gun on him.

"If I knew you were planning to kill me I wouldn't have come," Remo said.

The two holding the Russian rifles laughed at this and Charlie told them to shut up.

Remo was standing in a large metal steer bin 12 feet from the platform where Mary stood, an electronic prod in her hand. Charlie stood by her, playing with a large plastic thing with a metal tip that looked like a pointed dildo.

The other three were positioned to the sides and back of Remo, holding their weapons low and tight.

Remo had arrived in Vine Square after three different sets of directions.

The bell captain had said: "Go straight through on the interstate until you get to exit 277, then take route 664 south until you come to a fork in the road. Then just follow the signs and you can't miss it."

When Remo got off exit 277 and there was no route 664, he received the following:

"Well, acourse not. You go due no-arth here until ya git to Malpaso Road. You go raht they-uh and go strite on until ya reach Vahn Squay-uh. Ya cain't miss it."

And when Malpaso Road was a dead end to the right, "Take a left, then another left, go down two blocks, take a right. Then ask directions. You can't miss it."

Remo found it on the way to asking directions. He had expected a steaming factory full of fat cows but when he arrived, the yards and corrals were empty. An ominous silence hung over the white factory swirling in the hot Texas mists.

Remo jumped a fence into the muddy yard. By the time he had gotten 10 feet however, his shoes were unrecognizable blocks of mud. So he took them off, hopped up onto a fence, and walked along that until he reached an entrance normally used for the delivery of grain.

He noticed the clear, sparkling eye of a closed-circuit camera following him from the top of the high truck portal, but he did not look at it.

Remo entered and the glass lens hummed after him.

Mary Beriberi and Charlie Ko were in the control room watching Remo's progress on TV. It was a small room, totally encircled by video screens and the controls for the cameras that picked up almost everything in the slaughterhouse.

Mary had looked carefully at the "East-Side — outdoors" screen when Remo had hopped onto the fence.

"We take no chances," she said. "We get him where we want him first."

Charlie Ko had nodded, pulling a map of the entire factory from under his jacket.

Remo began to whistle *Anything Goes*. As he walked through the truck entrance Charlie had said, "Positions everybody. Sector eight. We've got the fucker."

Remo moved through the grain room, climbed up a conveyor belt, and went through a small hole in the roof.

"Make that sector six," yelled Charlie Ko. "He's not taking the stairs."

Remo got out of the hole to skip across several feeding bins.

"Uh..." Charlie checked the map. "We still have him in sector six. He's got to take the door."

But Remo did not take the door. Instead, he suddenly jumped against the wall, put his hands over his head, and dropped down a feed chute.

"Sector four! Down below! Hell, did you see that?"

Mary had to switch on the lower-level video cameras to tune Remo in again.

He was swinging from water pipe to water pipe. He swung until he was directly in front of a camera.

"This is a lot of fun," came his voice from the speaker below the screen. "But I don't have all day. What's my choice? The curtain or what's behind the door?"

Mary grinned wickedly. "Damn sure of yourself, aren't you, fucker?" She stabbed the microphone button on the console desk and said, "Keep going until you get to the door on the other side of the room. Go up one flight of stairs. We'll meet you there. Any more showing off and the girl dies."

The little red light atop all the videotape cameras winked out.

"You're not nice," Remo had said, moving toward the stairwell on the other side of the room.

"Don't move," Mary said. "One little, tiny gesture and we blast you. Nothing. Don't even scratch."

"I'm not even itchy," said Remo. "Mary. What's the Third World going to think? What happened to helping the helpless, defending the poor, protecting the downtrodden, and fighting for rights?"

"The Third World doesn't pay as good."

Someone behind Remo giggled. Charlie Ko told him to shut up.

"So you're the head of all this?" said Remo.

"No," said Mary Beriberi Greenscab. "I'm not, Mister Wise Guy Showoff. But I soon will be. By the time this nation recovers from the meat-eaters holocaust, I will be."

"O.K., fine, I'll buy that," said Remo. "So what are you waiting for? Shoot me and take over the country."

"Oh, no," said Mary, smiling. "First you are going to tell us how much you know and then you are going to die from a swine-flu shot reaction."

"All right," said Remo, sitting down in the big metal bin as if he were warming up to a Boy Scout fire. "You can find out how much I know from what I don't know. For instance, you are the ones putting the poison in the meat."

"Yes."

"The Pennsylvania convention?"

"Yes."

"The skeletons in the trees?"

"Yes."

"Why?" asked Remo.

"I'm sorry?"

"Why so much fooling around? The convention, then the skeletons, skinning bodies. What's the matter? You get bored easy? Why not just go ahead and poison the country?"

"Tests," said Mary simply. "At first our poison didn't work fast enough. So we tried it out on that convention and studied its effects.

"While we were working on a better mixture, a couple of people were getting close, like Angus and you. So we killed them according to traditional ritual. Now the poison is fast and 100 percent effective. We're going to start killing meat eaters by the millions."

Sheng Wa laughed. Charlie Ko told him to shut up.

"Traditional ritual?" asked Remo.

"Yes, Mr. Nichols. Didn't you know? We're honorary Chinese vampires. It is our creed to do away with all who desecrate the sacred stomach."

Now everyone started to laugh. Except Remo. He remembered what Chiun had said and felt a chill. He didn't think it was very funny. His voice cut off the levity.

"I don't understand this and I don't care." He got up. "You're all about to become just so much more meat." Remo heard the tone of his voice and was surprised that he sounded angry. Screw it. Screw his anger, and screw Chiun's fears, and screw Smith's detective work.

Remo was preparing his ankles and toes to send him up 12 feet into the air when the floor dropped out. He had been so angry that he didn't fully register Charlie's movement. Ko had pressed the pointed tube against the metal of the bin which had sent an electronic impulse to an automatic switch which opened the trapdoor floor.

Remo's toes curled, his legs twanged, but there was no longer anything to react against. He dropped like a stone.

Remo turned his muscles limp so no bones would be broken if he hit anything. He felt a gently sloping wall press into his side and he realized that he was now sliding along a chute.

A split second before he went through it, he saw a rectangular hole appear before him. Suddenly he was lying on the floor of a massive freezer.

A thick sheet of concrete-reinforced steel slid down over the entrance. Just before it locked Remo thought he heard hysterical laughter from above.

Remo looked around, bringing his body temperature down closer to that of the air around him. He estimated it at five degrees below zero. The walls were white-and-gray frozen slabs stretching down for 50 feet. The room was 20 feet wide, big enough to hold several dozen men working on the large carcasses of meat that were even now hung on hooks that lined the ceiling along the center of the freezer.

Remo walked down the line of dead cows to find the door. Then he heard a hissing sound. He looked down the row of carcasses to see a white cloud billowing out of a freezer unit, filling the other end of the room.

A smoke? A mist? Chiun's fears? It couldn't be. No, it couldn't be. But still, Remo began to move back, away from the gathering fog.

Remo started peering between sides of beef as he went, wondering why you could never find a cross when you needed one. And how to ward off a Chinese vampire? A cross made of chopsticks? A ring of wonton around your neck? Sprinkle soy sauce on their graves? Impale them on a fortune cookie?

Remo suddenly realized that the hunk of meat on his right looked different out the corner of his eye. It was a different color. It was a different shape. It was smaller.

And it had legs.

Remo turned. Viki Angus was on a meat hook. Her brown eyes were open and icicles had formed on her lower eyelids where her tears had frozen. Her mouth was open and her tongue had become a solid block of ice. Her head did not loll back because her neck was stiff and cold.

The hook protruded out the middle of her chest, just to the left of her silver Star Trek insignia. It was big and sharp and rounded and its slick black color clashed with the blue of her uniform. The other hooks were metal gray but this one was black because a thin layer of her blood had frozen on it before it had a chance to drip off.

Her body did not sway, her legs did not dangle. Her boots were on but her pantyhose were missing. They must have had fun with her before she died.

Remo stood before her silent corpse. He reached up to take her down and her frozen arm broke off in his hand.

Then the mist was upon him.

Mary Beriberi Greenscab was sitting with her feet up in the control room.

"It's too bad they don't have a camera in the freezer," said Charlie Ko, wistfully, playing with his fingernail. He was slicing pieces of paper in half that he threw into the air.

"The lens would freeze up, maybe break," said Mary, pulling her jeans-enclosed legs off the counter. She stood up and straightened her green checked shirt.

"So what's the gab, Greenscab?" said Sheng Wa.

"Yeah, what's hairy, Beriberi?" said Eddie Cantlie.

Everybody laughed until Mary flared, "Don't call me that. I don't need that cover anymore. My name is Broffman. Ms. Mary Broffman. But soon you can call me Ms. President." Mary smiled, sticking her thumbs under her lapels, and everyone in the control room hooted.

"Alright," she said. "This is it. Yat-Sen and Gluck should be back any minute. You guys go get Nichols and Angus. Thaw them both out. Drop Nichols anywhere and stick the girl with the old chink in a tree." Mary moved toward the exit door.

"Hey," said Charlie Ko. "What are you going to do?"

Mary turned back. "I? I? I am going to report 'mission accomplished' to the leader. Then I'm going to the airport."

Charlie's eyes widened. "You're going to drop the stuff?"

Mary smiled. "By tonight, the meat eaters will be dropping like flies. By next week, we'll have this government on its knees."

Mary left. The boys howled and hooted.

"All right," said Charlie, taking over. "Let's get this place cleaned up. I'll call Texas Solly and tell him he can open up again tomorrow. If he's still around tomorrow."

The group moved down into the slaughterhouse disassembly line. They moved across a metal balcony which led onto a spiral staircase that moved down into the huge room proper. The chutes, machinery, and monorail-like harness for the steers were clean and unmoving. The chutes and trap doors where the dead cows appeared lined one wall. A battery of opaque windows lined another. Benches and work tables were underneath the second-story balcony and the huge door to the freezer occupied the fourth and facing wall.

Sheng Wa and Steinberg moved in front of the cold-storage entrance as Eddie Cantlie came down the stairs. Charlie Ko moved across the edge of the railed balcony overlooking the entire floor.

Steinberg turned back from the door and looked up at Charlie.

"How do you open this damn thing anyway?"

They didn't have to.

There was a cracking whump and suddenly the entire freezer door broke off from the wall and went flying across the room. Sheng Wa and Steinberg were in its path so they were smacked forward to smash against the wall and drop onto the work tables like rag dolls before the still-flying door crushed them into powder.

Charlie Ko saw the huge floor disappear under him before he heard the sickening crash. Then he looked back to the now-open entrance as a huge cloud of cold air and white mist billowed into the room.

The puffy billows built up like smoke bombs at a rock-and-roll show or a nuclear explosion climbing the sky until a figure came leaping out from the very heart of the cloud. A dark-haired, thin man with thick wrists came bounding up into the room.

Remo Williams, the Destroyer, soul intact, dropped lightly to the floor as the smoke swirled around him.

Charlie dropped to his knees, his mouth open, his knuckles white gripping the protective railing, and Eddie Cantlie had fallen back on the stairs, staring at him between two rungs of the banister.

And Remo intoned, "I am created Shiva the Destroyer, the dead night tiger made whole by Sinanju. What is this dog meat that now stands before me?"

Eddie Cantlie felt his pants go wet and he tried to scramble back up the stairs. Remo walked over and punched the bottom stair. The entire revolving stairwell began to vibrate. Remo punched it again. The stairs began to shake until the internal strength of the steel could no longer stand the unnatural vibration and began to break up.

Remo took a step back and lightly tapped the bottom stair with his heel, as if by an afterthought. The top stair disconnected from the balcony. The bottom stair ripped up from the floor and the entire structure toppled with Eddie Cantlie in the middle.

Eddie seemed to hover momentarily in the air as the heavy stairwell crashed to the floor. He collided with the banister, then the structure bounced. Eddie hit the center beam, then bounced himself to fall face first on the concrete floor. He never felt the floor.

Remo turned to Charlie. Charlie turned to run and then screamed. Before him stood Chiun. In each hand Chiun held large liquid-looking bean bags. Except these bean bags had faces. They were stretched and lumpy faces, as if every bone in them had been squashed into sand, but still, they were faces. They were Yat-Sen and Gluck's faces. Charlie Ko fell to his knees.

Chiun looked down at Charlie and then to the two hulks he held in his hands. He screwed his face in disgust.

"Amateur help," he said. Then he threw his two human bean bags over the railing onto the floor before Remo. They hit the ground without bouncing. They just wiggled like so much jello.

"Don't kill that one," Remo called up. "I need to talk to him."

"The others are not dead," said Chiun. "I brought them here to be killed by you. It is written that Shiva shall put down the second coming of the undead and my ancestor's disgrace."

Remo looked at the two blobs of barely existing matter that lay before him. He could not imagine how Chiun had managed to walk through downtown Houston with one on the end of each hand.

"Where does it say that Shiva will put down the undead?" he asked.

"It is written," said Chiun. "But do not worry. They are not truly of the undead."

"How do you know?"

"They entered my room unbidden. I was deep in the throes of the

Final Death when they came in without permission. It was then that I realized that they could not be truly of the Creed."

Remo remembered when the mist came over him in the freezer. Chiun must have done what he had done when he realized that he had been tricked. Remo remembered how his stomach knotted and numbness had crept throughout his body.

It was the same sensation he had the last two times he had been poisoned. So he did what he did then. He upped the oxygen content in his blood to assimilate the poison. Then he concentrated his entire essence on his stomach. The center of all life and death. Then when all the oxygen and blood and poison rushed into his stomach, he threw it up and out.

In the freezer now was a little pile of frozen green, red and black. Just below Viki Angus's broken body.

Remo kneeled down on one knee between the quivering piles of Yat-Sen and Gluck.

"I'd like to make this painful, guys, but I don't have the time."

He drove the first knuckle of each hand into their respective heads. What was left of their respective heads. He felt his digits sink deep into their whole and intact brains. Then he threw their carcasses into the freezer to join the puke.

Remo looked up to where Chiun stood before a quaking Charlie Ko. Remo's eyes met the old man's and there flashed an emotion between them. It was the love of father for son, and son for father.

Charlie Ko made his move. His legs straightened and he whipped his long-nailed right forefinger out in front of his hurtling body directly in line with the soft, thin, unprotected layer of flesh below Chiun's jaw. He felt the solid rush of adrenalin that came from knowing that he could take the old man's head clean off.

If it was still there to take. Suddenly the yellow body before him was gone and Charlie felt himself flying through empty air. Then there was a yellow flash from below, a tug at his wrist, and Charlie Ko stopped in midair on his feet.

His hand didn't. His hand still with his forefinger out, still with his other four fingers clenched, spun across the metal balcony, teetered on the edge, and dropped over.

Blood began to spurt out of his right arm stump as Remo leaped up onto the balcony and gripped the back of Charlie's neck and his right forearm in such a way that the bleeding stopped but the blinding pain didn't.

"Okay, fella," Remo said. "You want to talk now or wait till after lunch?"

Charlie poured out his soul, knowing that this was the end and that, somehow, his talking would make the incredible pain end more quickly.

"We were hired by this old man to kill every nonvegetarian in the country."

"How?"

"We used this two-part poison the old man gave us. One part went into the meat, one part went into the gas."

"Why?"

"Because the authorities would have been able to locate the poison easily and develop an antidote if any one part were toxic. The part in the meat is kind of weak. But the gas activates it, makes it deadly."

"How did you get it in the meat?"

"Eddie... he was the one on the stairs. He was the government inspector at this plant. We put it in the USDA ink."

Smith had been right. Remo returned his attentions to Charlie.

"Where's Mary?"

"She went to report to the leader."

Chiun looked at Remo.

"Where's he?"

"At the Sheraton. Room 1824."

"Good year. Anything else?"

"Yeah, yeah. Mary is going to the airport and spread the gas over the city."

Remo dropped Charlie in disgust. The pain behind his neck stopped, but the blood started coursing out of his stump again.

"Come on, Little Father, let's go," said Remo.

"No, my son, you must kill the man yourself."

Remo turned back. "Why?"

"It is written that you will deliver the blow that avenges my father's disgrace."

"Where does it say that?"

"Just do it," spat Chiun. "Must you always bicker?"

Remo moved toward Chiun and Charlie's contorting body. "How many times do I have to go through this thing?" he complained. "Every time we get a new assignment, it's written here that I'll do this, it's written there that I'll do that. Can't we just go?"

"It is written," said Chiun. "That the son of the son of the father must do the deed."

"I never read that," said Remo. "Was that part of the fine print?"

Charlie Ko looked up at the two and screeched, "Please."

"All right," said Remo. "If you put it that way." He moved in and with one stroke ended Charlie's torture permanently.

Chiun beamed. "My son, I am proud of you."

"Proud?" said Remo. "You're proud of me? Proud? Of me, the white man, the pale piece of pig's ear?"

"Well, perhaps proud is a little excessive," Chiun said. "Highly tolerant is more correct. After all, it has been many days and still my manuscript is not delivered onto television. Important things like that are not easily forgotten."

Remo sighed.

"And another thing. Your wrist was bent when you disposed of that garbage."

"Oh God, here we go again. He's dead, isn't he?"

"Dead is dead and wrong is wrong," said Chiun. "Why was your wrist bent?"

"I'll explain it all to you on the way to the airport," Remo said.

CHAPTER THIRTEEN

IT WAS A BEAUTIFUL DAY for flying. The sky was clear, the visibility was 50 miles and the sun was slowly sinking in the west.

The golden strands of sunset were just beginning to reach across the horizon when Ms. Mary Broffman radioed the control tower and asked permission for take-off.

She had told the leader of their success with the two agents of Sinanju, then prepared herself for the flight of the Final Death.

She had refilled the gasoline tank on her orange-and-white two-seater, specially fitted Piper Cub airplane, nicknamed "hojo" because when it was flying it resembled a Howard Johnson's restaurant with its orange roof. Then she had checked all her gauges and shifts, then the engine and flaps, then the little motorcycle motor attached to the dull-green canister in back.

All was in readiness. By nightfall most of the meat eaters in Texas would heel over. And by the morning the country would be in panic. Bodies would be littering the streets. The government would probably be gutted piecemeal. Large corporations would be leaderless and hollow. All manufacturing would grind to a halt. The entire foundation of the country would crumble.

Those left would be helpless wanderers. For a precious few days before the entire hemisphere was quarantined and the gas wore off before the first of the doubtless many foreign attacks that would be launched to lay siege on the fat, dead nation, there would be time. Time to accumulate riches beyond belief. Wealth beyond measure.

And then to pilot another plane to another land, where the secret of the two-part poison would lead to incredible power and position.

The leader was a fool to entrust this vegetarian wonder to his "followers." By morning he too would be dead. Mary would see to it. And then there would be no one between her, and whatever she wanted. Not bad for a little girl from Staten Island. If someone had told her five years ago that she would have reached this position simply from interviewing a Chinese gentleman in a library for her China history course, she would not have believed it.

But here she was. Minutes away from total, absolute freedom. "Piper Cub Z-112, you are cleared for take-off on runway three. Have a good flight. Over."

"Thank you, control. Am starting engines to take off on runway three. Over."

Mary started her engines. The extra-horsepower Volkswagen engine in front of her sputtered, caught, and roared to life. She felt the vibration in the joystick between her legs and enjoyed the rush it always gave. Grass bent in the whirling propeller's wake. Dust was kicked up and swirled behind her.

An old, blind Chinaman in a library. A rich Jewish girl who needed a quick interview to finish a report for a school she was to drop out of two months later. An alliance formed between a desperate man and a bored girl. An incredible adventure shared in life and death. And it all came to this. The total, mind-blowing power of having the fate of the entire nation behind you attached to a motorcycle motor.

The orange-and-white airplane began to move. Mary pushed the throttle forward and began to bump down the asphalt to runway three for her first sweep.

Dusk was descending so she switched on her red-and-white flashers to warn any approaching aircraft of her presence. The runway lights glowed in the distance and the airport floodlights suddenly switched on.

Mary turned the plane around to face down runway three for her first sweep to gain momentum and power for liftoff. And in the glare of the airport lights, down on runway eight, a man hopped over the fence.

Mary began to inch forward. She looked toward the small human shape in the distance moving across the field in her general direction. The plane picked up momentum as she picked up her radio microphone.

"Control, control, this is Cub Z-112. There's a man on the field. I repeat, there is a man on the field. Over."

There were a few crackling moments of radio silence, then the tiny speaker over her head replied.

"Z-112, this is control. Where? I repeat where is the man? Over."

Mary's plane was rolling down the runway at a steady clip now. She turned to look down the field and saw what was definitely a man moving in a straight line across runway seven.

"Control, this is Z-112. The man is crossing runway seven. I repeat, runway seven. Do you read? Over."

Another few seconds passed, as if the control-tower man had stopped to carefully survey the field. Mary stole another look to see the man moving onto runway six. She could now see that his right arm was up in the air.

"Z-112, this is control. I see no man on runway seven. I repeat, no man on runway seven. Over."

Mary had reached the end of her first run and was sweeping around for her final taxiing for take-off.

"Control, this is Z-112," said Mary, her voice strangely tight. "He's there, control. I see him. He has just crossed runway six. I repeat, just crossed runway six. Over."

Mary stared out her window to her left now as she saw the man moving in a diagonal as if to cut her off. She could see that he was carrying something in his raised right hand. And that something was dripping.

"Z-112, this is control. I still cannot see a man on the field. Have you been drinking? I repeat, have you been drinking? Over."

"Idiot," spat Mary. "I have not been drinking and he's there, damn it. I can see him as clear as day. Are you blind or something? Look, look, he's crossing runway five."

Mary turned and saw the man coming toward runway three. His head was turned in her direction and she saw his dark hair and high cheek bones. She saw that he was wearing a black T-shirt, blue slacks, and that he was barefoot.

In his hand was a bloody meat hook.

"Z-112, this is control. I have checked with several members of the ground crew as well as double checking myself, and we can still see no man on the runway. You had better taxi back for inspection. I repeat, taxi back for inspection."

"Like hell," Mary screamed. "The lousy fucker's on the field and he's coming after me."

Mary revved up her engine full and thrust her throttle down. The plane leaped down the runway. She watched the speedometer climb and grinned, picturing the dark-haired man trying to catch up with her but left standing in all the flying dirt, pebbles, exhaust, and garbage her engine threw behind the plane.

She took a quick glance out of her window and felt a hammer blow in her stomach. He was still gaining on her. She watched in horrified amazement as he loped across runway four, the meat hook held up like the Olympic torch, at the summer Montreal games.

He seemed to be moving very slowly but his form just kept getting bigger and clearer.

Mary quickly looked at the speedometer. She was just a few kilometers below take-off velocity. Just a few more seconds and she'd beat him. If she could just keep moving for a few more seconds...

Suddenly Mary laughed wildly. What was she getting hysterical about? Let him catch up with the plane. What was he going to do? Kick her? Trip her with the hook? At this velocity, even if he somehow managed to throw the metal into her propeller, it would probably just bounce off and do very little damage.

So let him catch up. Let him run into the plane. Let him get mashed against the side. Let him get sliced into cold cuts. Come on, Mr. Wise Guy Superman. Come and get it.

Mary had reached take-off velocity. She felt her stomach settle as the wheels of the plane left the ground. She saw the airfield drop away from her windshield.

She laughed again and looked back in triumph. The man had

stopped growing larger. Mary smirked. But now the hook was getting larger. Mary suddenly lost her sense of humor.

She ignored the swirling sunset out the front as she watched, in dread fascination. The hook seemed to float alongside the plane in slow motion. It turned slowly in the air, getting bigger and bigger. Then it was life-size right in front of her face.

Then her view shattered. There was a cracking scream and then a violent pressure, as if someone had dropped a barbell on her chest. She watched as every loose object in her plane broke loose in the rush of wind. She watched her flight plan fly up, her silver chromatic two-color pen, her sunglasses and her leather attaché case. She saw her auburn hair streak across her vision and she slowly wondered why her seat belt had not snapped so she would be sucked out too.

She held on tightly to the throttle and looked down. Coming out of her stomach was the tail end of a meat hook.

The point and catch of the metal had rammed through her body and locked out the back of her pilot's seat.

Mary threw her head back and howled like a drowning wolf. She opened her eyes and saw the horizon stretched out in front of her in a slash. From the top left of her broken windshield to the bottom right. Like the edge of a guillotine blade. Like the edge of the leader's fingernail.

Then the ground filled her vision and then nothing. She did not even have the time to feel pain. She did not even see the engine explode into the cockpit with the raging force of a full tank of gas. She did not even know that when the airport emergency crew put out the fire at the end of runway three and found what was left of her body that the meat hook looked like just another piece of melted metal.

She never knew that when the dull green canister melted, the fire evaporated the white mist immediately. She never knew that the control-tower man reported to the board of inquiry that she had shown signs of drunkenness and hysteria just before take-off.

And she never knew that the man who had come across five runways to get to her, the man who could move his body in such a way that light did not reflect off it toward the control tower, the man who could move so that he would never be where any member of the ground crew was looking, the man who had hurled the cold, bloody meat hook into her cockpit, had stood by the burning, wrecked carcass of her plane just after it had crashed, spread his arms and said, "That's the biz, sweetheart."

CHAPTER FOURTEEN

"IT'S DONE, OH LEADER," said a voice in room 1824, the Houston Sheraton. "The meat eaters have gone to their Final Deaths."

The leader gripped the heads of the green-fanged dragon arm rests in supplication. He had waited, for what seemed like eons, for those very words to be spoken. He would not worry if they were not spoken by his female translator's voice as he had expected. For they were spoken in Chinese. And they were spoken.

The male voice had said that the stomach desecrators had gone on to their Final Deaths. Which meant that now he could go on to his last reward. He could enter the afterlife and join his ancestors, his loved ones and companions. His gamble had paid off. The doubt of entrusting his creed's age-old secrets to paid mercenaries was over. They had done their jobs. The objective of their creed had been achieved. The leader sighed.

"It is good," he said.

"No," said a high-pitched Oriental voice in another tongue. "It is not good. It is evil."

The leader knew the language. It was Korean.

Remo and Chiun stood before the blood-red chair and its wizened occupant in the darkened hotel suite. One overhead 40 watt bulb shone down between the three, bathing their faces in dim, yellow light.

The leader tensed and sucked in his breath.

"Sinanju," he exhaled.

"Yes," said Chiun. "And your turn has come."

The leader's white brows came together in a V, the lines in his face deepened, then he relaxed and smiled.

"It shall be as it is," he said, waving a hand. "But surely you must understand. You, who live by a belief as old as mine. You must know the honor and dedication that drove me on."

Chiun shook his head gravely. "Sinanju is not a belief," he intoned. "It is a way of life. A way of life we do not force onto others. Few are blessed with the honor that is Sinanju." The Master looked at Remo. "We would not have it any other way."

"So it is not done," said the leader with sudden apprehension.

"No, it is not," said Chiun. "The only ones cursed with the Final Death are your amateur help."

The Korean leaned in to hiss into the leader's ear.

"You could have finished us as easily as drowning a child. Yea, as old and blind as you are. You had only to face us yourself and your creed could have ruled the earth again."

The Master rose to his full height.

"But you diluted your wisdom with the stupidity of others until you were no more dangerous than a dying wind. So now you must pay."

"Yes," said the leader, anxious to join his creed in the afterlife. "I am ready. Do it now. Kill me."

Chiun stepped back. "Yes, you will die," he said. "But we will not kill you. For you are of the undead, and it is written that only in death are you truly alive. So it follows that only in life are you truly dead."

The leader sat still, drinking in Chiun's words. Then, before the full meaning of those words dawned on him, before he could drive his own fingernail into his neck to escape, Remo moved.

His right hand chopped just under the leader's ear, stopping all movement, paralyzing all limbs as the left hand sped forward, faster than the eye could follow, faster than skin could react, faster than bone could break, to snake into the leader's skull, to shave a part of the leader's brain, then withdraw, without stopping movement to join the right hand again at Remo's side.

The leader still sat. No cut appeared on his skin. No break could be discerned upon his skull. His eyes were closed, but the heart still beat, the blood still flowed, the mind still worked.

But the electrical impulses that guided the muscles went no further than the top of his spine. The leader's mind no longer had any direct control of his body. The brain still functioned but his limbs would not respond to his orders. He was trapped.

"See?" said Remo to Chiun. "I didn't bend my wrist that time."

The Houston doctors marveled at the patient. The old Chinese was almost an exact replica of the case of the Massachusetts girl who had been in a coma since birth.

He, like she, was still alive, but he, like she was unaware of that fact. An incredible case. The Houston doctors were pleased and honored to get it.

They had warned the man who committed him that there was very little chance of his ever recovering.

"That's all right," said the man. "Just keep my grandfather alive as long as possible."

They had warned the man that with the new life-sustaining techniques, it was quite conceivable that the old Oriental could outlive them all.

"That's fine," said the man. "I'd like to think of him as a memorial to the family."

They had warned the man that this sort of prolonged treatment would be very expensive.

"That's fine too," said the man, plopping down five piles of hundred dollar bills. "Money is no object."

The doctors had no more warnings. After they checked the authenticity of the bills, they hoped that Mr. Nichols' grandfather would live a long and full life in the intensive-care unit and that Mr. Nichols and his father would visit any time they pleased.

"Well, actually," said Remo, "we're going out of town for a long time. Just, please, keep granddaddy alive."

The doctors sympathized and wished Mr. Nichols and his father well, even though they could not figure out how, medically speaking, a tall, white, dark-haired American was born to such a short, white-haired, yellow-skinned man.

Remo and Chiun left the Houston Hospital to go back to their hotel.

"I'm glad you did not pay gold," Chiun said. "Chinamen aren't worth it."

"Paper will do," said Remo. "Besides, I'm going to have a wonderful time explaining to Smitty why we needed the money in the first place."

"Tell him we will return it. It will gladden the emperor's heart," Chiun said.

"And just how do you propose we do that?" Remo asked. "That was $25,000. A lot of scratch."

"It is as nothing compared to all that you will earn next week when you deliver my daytime drama to the television people. It will make me wealthy. And your three percent share as my agent will enable you to repay Smith."

"My what?"

"Your four percent share," said Chiun.

"My what?"

"Your five percent share," said Chiun, coldly, then turned away and told the wall: "All agents are bandits."

THE END

EXCERPT

If you enjoyed *The Final Death*, maybe you'll like *Mugger Blood*, too. It's
the thirtieth (and grittiest!) *Destroyer* novel, and is now available as an
ebook and in paperback.

Mugger Blood

HIS NAME WAS REMO and he was taking the elevator up — from beneath.
He smelled the heavy buildup of engine fumes embedded in the caked
grease, and felt long cables tremble ever so slightly when the elevator
came to a floor and that fifteen-story ripple started with a halt of the
elevator and shimmied down to the basement and then back up past
the fifteenth floor to the penthouse, five stories overhead.

He had a good forearm hold on a bolt that he kept just above his
lean frame. People who held onto things for their lives usually tired
quickly, precisely because they held on for their lives. Fear gave speed
and power to the muscles, not endurance.

If one wanted to hold onto something, one became a solid part of it,
extended himself out through the extruding bolt, so that the grip did
not strangle but extended from what it was joined to. As he had been
taught, he let the hand do the attaching lightly and forgot about it. So
that when the elevator started again, his body swayed easily from the
hand that was the pivot joint and up he went.

It was his right hand and he could hear people walking just above
his right ear.

He had been there since early morning and when the elevator
stopped at the penthouse floor, he knew he would not be there much
longer. At the penthouse floor, different things happened. Remo heard
locks snap, twenty stories down, twenty locks, each for an elevator
door. He had been told about this. He heard the grunt of muscled men

who forced themselves up through strain. They checked the top of the elevator. He had been told about that also. The bodyguards always checked the roof of the elevator because it was known men could hide there.

The roof was sealed with reinforced steel plating and so was the floor. This prevented anyone from burrowing down or up into the elevator.

The elevator to the street was the only vulnerable point in the penthouse complex of the South Korean consul in Los Angeles. The rest was a fortress. Remo had been told about that.

And when he was asked how he would penetrate this complex, he answered that he was paid for his services, not his wisdom. Which was true. But even truer was that Remo did not really know how he was going to penetrate this complex at the time and he didn't feel like thinking about it, and most of all, he hadn't felt like carrying on the conversation. So he threw out some wiseacre comment, the kind he himself had endured for more than a decade, and on the morning that Upstairs wanted the job done, he sauntered over to the building with the elegant penthouse fortress and made his first move without even thinking.

One did not have to scheme too much anymore. At first, the defenses he had run into — where people locked gates or lived high up or surrounded themselves with bodyguards — had presented problems. And it was very exciting at first to solve them.

This morning, for some reason, he had been thinking about daffodils. He had seen some earlier in the spring and this morning he was thinking about these yellow flowers and how now when he smelled them, it was entirely different from the way he had smelled them before, before he had become this other person he now was. In the old days, there might have been a sweet odor. But now when he smelled a flower, he could inhale its movements. It was a symphony of pollen climaxing in his nostrils. It was a chorus and a shout of life. To be Sinanju, to be a learner and a knower of the disciplines of the small North Korean village on the West Korean Bay was to know life more fully. A second now had more life in it than an hour had had before.

Of course, sometimes Remo didn't want more life. He would have preferred less of it.

So, thinking of these yellow flowers, he entered the new white brick-and-aluminum building with the full story-high windows and the elegant marble entranceway and the waterfall going over the plastic flowers in the lobby, took the elevator up to the tenth floor. There, he fiddled around with the stop and emergency buttons until he got the tenth floor about waist-high, then slid under the elevator, found a bolt on the undercarriage, locked his right hand to it, until amid screaming from many floors, someone got the elevator started again. And there he waited and swung until later when the elevator went all the way up to the penthouse.

Not much thinking. He had been told so early by his teacher, by Chiun, current Master of Sinanju, that people always show you the best way to attack them.

If they have a weakness, they surround it with ditches or armor plating or bodyguards. So Remo, upon hearing of all the protection around the elevator when he got the assignment, went right to the elevator, thinking of daffodils because there wasn't really much else to think about.

And now, the person he wanted walked into the elevator, asking questions in Korean. Were all the locks on so the trip down could not be interrupted? They were, Colonel. Was the top hatch secure? Yes, Colonel. The roof entrance? Yes, Colonel. The floor? Yes, Colonel. And Colonel, you look so splendid in your gray suit.

Most American, no?

Yes, like a businessman.

It is all business.

Yes, Colonel.

And the twenty stories of cable moved.

And the elevator lowered.

And Remo rocked his body. The elevator descending in a long slow drop of twenty stories rocked with the light human form on its undercarriage, like a bell with a swinging dapper. It picked up the back-and-forth of the rhythm-perfect sinew machine on its undercarriage, and at the twelfth floor, the elevator began banging its guide rails, spitting sparks and shivering the inside panels.

The occupants pressed emergency stop. The coils snapped to a quivering stillness. Remo took three slow swings, and on the third hand-ladled his body up into the floor space at the door opening above him, and then, getting his left hand up into the rubber of the inner elevator door, gave the whole sliding mechanism a good bang and a healthy shove with his left side.

The door opened like a champagne cork popping into an aluminum cradle. And Remo was inside the elevator.

"Hello," he said in his most polite Korean but he knew, even with his heavy American accent, the tones of the greeting were sodden with the heaviness of the northern Korean town of Sinanju, the only accent Remo had ever learned.

The short Korean with the lean hard face had a .38 Police Special out of the shoulder holster under his blue jacket with good speed. It told Remo that the man in the gray was definitely the colonel and the one he wanted. Koreans, when they had bodyguards, thought it beneath their dignity to fight. And this was somewhat strange because the colonel was supposed to be one of the most deadly men in the south of that country with both hand and knife, and, if he wished, the gun too.

"I don't suppose that would pose any problem to you?" Remo had been asked when given the assignment and told of the colonel's skills.

"Nah," Remo had said.

"He has the renowned black belt in karate," Remo had been told.

"Yeah, hmmm," Remo had said, not all that interested.

"Would you like to see his moves in action then?"

"Nah," Remo had said.

"He is perhaps one of the most feared men in Asia. He is very close to South Korea's president. We need him alive. He's a fanatic so that may not be easy." This warning had come from Dr. Harold W. Smith, director of Folcroft Sanitarium, the cover for a special organization which worked outside the laws of the land, in the hope that the rest of the system could work inside. Remo was its silent enforcement arm and Chiun the teacher who had given him more than American money could buy.

For while the assassins of Sinanju had rented out their services to emperors and kings and pharaohs even before the Western world started keeping track of years by numbers, they never sold how they did it.

So when the organization paid for Chiun to teach Remo to kill, they got their money's worth. But when Chiun taught Remo to breathe and live and think and explore the inner universe of his own body, creating a creature that used its brain cells and body organs at least eight times more effectively than normal man, Chiun gave the secret organization more than it had bargained for. A new man, totally different from the one sent to him for training.

And Remo could not explain it. He could not tell Smith what the teachings of Sinanju had given him; it would be like trying to explain soft to someone who could not feel, or red to a person born blind. You did not explain Sinanju and what the masters knew and taught to someone who was going to ask you someday if you might have trouble with a karate expert. Does the winter have trouble with the snow? Someone who thought of Remo's watching movies of another fighter in action could not possibly understand Sinanju. Ever.

But Smith had insisted upon showing the movies of the colonel in action. It was taken by the CIA, which had worked heavily with the colonel at one time. Now there was a strain between Korea and America and the colonel was one of the larger parts of it. They could not get to him because he had become familiar with American weapons. It was like a teacher trying to trick an old pupil who had grown too wise. It was just the sort of mission Smith thought the organization would be good for.

"That's nice," Remo had said and whistled an off-key tune in the hotel room in Denver where he had gotten the assignment for the Korean colonel. Smith, undeterred by Remo's indifference that had blossomed into yawning boredom, ran the movies of the colonel in action. The colonel broke a few boards, kicked a few younger men in the jaw, and danced around a bit. The movie was black and white.

"Whew," Smith had said. He arched an eyebrow, a very severe emotion on that normally frosted face.

"Yeah, wha'?" asked Remo. What was Smith talking about?

"I couldn't see his hands," said Smith.

"Not that fast," said Remo. After a while you had to listen and observe people to find out where their limits were, because sometimes you just couldn't believe how dead they were to life. Smith really believed the man was fast and dangerous, Remo realized.

"His hands were a blur," said Smith.

"Nah," said Remo. "Stop the frames where he's flailing around. They're sharp."

"You mean to tell me you can see individual frames in a movie?" asked Smith. "That's impossible."

"As a matter of fact, unless I remind myself to relax, that's all I see. It's all a bunch of stills."

"You couldn't see his hands in still frames," Smith challenged.

"All right, fine," said Remo pleasantly. If Smith wanted to believe that, fine. Was there anything else that Smith wanted?

Smith dimmed the lights in the hotel room and put the small movie projector into reverse. The lights flickered into a blur, as the camera whirred and then stopped. There was the still frame. And there was the colonel's striking hand, frozen and clear. Smith moved the camera still by still to another frame, then another. The hand was picture-sharp throughout, not too fast for the film at all.

"But it looked so fast," said Smith. So regularly and consistently had he acknowledged that Remo had changed that he was not aware of how much had truly happened, how much Remo had really changed.

And Remo told him more that he thought had changed. "When I first started doing all this for you, I used to respect what we were doing. No more," Remo had said, and he had left that hotel room with instructions on what America wanted from the Korean colonel. He could have had a few hours' briefing on how the CIA and the FBI had failed to reach the man, what his defenses were, but all he wanted was a general description of the building so he could find it. And, of course, Smitty had mentioned the protection on the elevator.

So Remo watched the .38 Special come around towards him from the man in the blue suit and watched the man in the gray suit back away to let his servant do the job and that was good enough identification for him.

He caught the gun wrist with a forefinger, snapping it through the bone. He did this in such perfect consonance with the bodyguard's own rhythm, it appeared as if the man had taken the gun out of the holster only to throw it away. The hand didn't stop moving and the gun flew into the open crack between floors and down into silence. As Remo cupped his hand behind the head, he gave his fingers and palms an extra little twist. This was not a stroke he had been taught. He wanted to wipe away the grease from the elevator's undercarriage. He did that as he brought the guard's head down into his rising knee — one, pushing through with a tidy snap at the end, right behind the man's head towards the open wall; two, caught the returning body; and three, put it to rest quietly and forever on its back.

"Hi, sweetheart," said Remo to the colonel in English. "I need your cooperation." The colonel threw his briefcase at Remo's head. It hit a wall and snapped open, spilling packages of green American money. Apparently the colonel was heading to Washington to either rent or buy an American congressman.

The colonel assumed a dragon position with arching hands like claws, and elbows forward. The colonel hissed. Remo wondered whether there were sales on American congressmen like any other commodity. Did one get the votes of a dozen congressmen cheaper than buying twelve separately? Was a vote ever reduced to a bargain? What was the price of a Supreme Court justice? And what about cabinet members? Could someone purchase something in a nice Secretary of Commerce?

The colonel kicked.

Or perhaps rent a director of the FBI? Could a buyer be interested in a vice president? They were really very cheap. The last one sold out for cash in an envelope, bringing disgrace to a White House already full of it. Imagine a vice president selling out for only fifty thousand dollars in cash payoff. That brought shame to his office and his country. For fifty thousand dollars, one should get no more than a vice president of Greece. It was a disgrace to be able to buy an American vice president for so little.

Remo caught the kick.

But what could one expect from anyone who would write a book for money?

The colonel threw a kick with the other leg, which Remo caught, and returned the foot to the floor. The colonel sent a stroke that could crush brick at Remo's skull. Remo caught the hand and put it back at the colonel's side. Then came the other hand, and back it went too.

Perhaps, thought Remo, American Express or Master Charge might simply credit an account, or every freshman congressman would get one of the stickers of those credit agencies and attach it to his office door and when someone wanted to bribe him, he wouldn't have to carry cash out into the dangerous Washington streets, but just present his credit card and the congressman could take out one of those machines he would get when he swore to uphold the Constitution as he took office, and run through the briber's credit card and at the end of every month get his bribe through his own bank. Just bribing a congressman with cold cash was demeaning.

The colonel bared his teeth and lunged, trying to get a bite at Remo's throat.

Possibly, thought Remo, there might even be a stock market for Washington politicians, with bids on farm votes and things like that. Senators up three points, congressmen down an eighth, the president steady. And while his thoughts were sarcastic, Remo was greatly sad. Because he did not want his government to be that, he did not want that stain of corruption, he not only wanted to believe in his country and his government, he wanted the facts to justify it also. It was not even good enough the majority were honest, he wanted all of them that way. And he hated the money strewn around this elevator floor as he throttled the Korean colonel. For that money was destined for American politicians and it meant that there were hands out.

So this little thing with the colonel was a bit of a pleasure and he leveled the man and put him on his back and very slowly he said — so that the man would be sure this was not just a windy threat — "Colonel, I am about to puree your face in my hands. You can save your face and your lungs, which can be snapped out of your body, and your gonads and various other parts of your body that you will miss tremendously. You can do this by cooperating. I am a busy man, Colonel."

And in Korean, the colonel gasped: "Who are you?"

"Would you believe a Freudian analyst?" asked Remo, pressing his right thumb under the colonel's cheekbone and pressing down so that the left eye of the colonel strained at its nerve endings.

"*Aieee*," screamed the colonel.

"And so, please dig deep into your subconscious and come up with your payroll of American politicians. All right, sweetie?" said Remo.

"*Aieeee,*" screamed the colonel, because it felt as if the eye were coming out of its socket.

"Very good," said Remo and released pressure. The eye eased back into the socket, suddenly filled with a roadmap of red veins as the burst capillaries flooded the eyeball. The red lines in the left eye would disappear in two days. And by the time they did, the colonel would be a defector in the custody of the FBI. He would be called a key witness and newsmen would say he defected because he was afraid of returning to South Korea, which of course made no sense for he was one of the closest friends of the South Korean president. And the colonel would name names and how much each one got.

And Remo hoped they would go to jail. It offended him that the grease-slicked head with the little rat grin of a former vice president went pandering around the world when he should have been behind bars doing time like the common thief he was.

So he told the colonel very clearly and very slowly in English and in Korean that all the names would be named and that there was nothing that could protect the colonel.

"Because, Colonel, I have greater access to your nerves and to your pain than you do," said Remo, as the elevator closed its door and descended towards the basement.

"Who are you?" asked the colonel, whose English occasionally lost verbs but who pronounced any figure above ten thousand dollars flawlessly. "You work for me. Fifty thousand dollars."

"You're not talking to a vice president of the United States," said Remo angrily.

"A hundred thousand."

"Nobody voted me into office, buddy," said Remo.

"Two hundred thousand. I make you rich. You work for me."

"You don't understand. I am not the director of the FBI. I've never sworn to uphold the Constitution and carry out any duties on behalf of the American people. I'm not for sale," said Remo and took one of the bundles of new one-hundred-dollar bills and put the edge of it into the colonel's mouth.

"Eat. It's good for you. Eat. Please. Just a nibble. Try it, you'll like it," said Remo, and as the colonel tried to chew at the corner of the paper Remo told him who he was.

"I'm the spirit of America, Colonel. The man who walked on the moon, who invented the light bulb, who grows more food on his land because of his own sweat than any other. If I have a fault, it's that I've been too kind to too many people too often. Eat."

When the elevator reached the lower security area and the door opened, the guards at the door saw only their commander leaning numbly against the back of the elevator and his bodyguard stretched dead upon the floor, his right hand loose jelly in unpunctured skin. Money was strewn around the elevator floor and for some strange reason, the colonel was chewing on the end of a packet of bills.

"Take me to the FBI immediately," he said in a daze.

When they were gone, Remo slid from the undercarriage where he had waited before and squirmed his way through a bread box-sized hole, out into the garage.

He heard people yelling all the way up the twenty stories of the building at the closed and locked elevator doors. He smiled at a startled guard.

By noon, Remo was back at the trim white yacht in San Francisco Bay that he had left early that morning. He moved quietly because he did not wish to disturb what was happening in the cabin. It sounded like iron pans being clanged against a blackboard. Remo waited outside and noticed that the sounds went on uninterrupted. It was Chiun reciting his poetry and usually he would stop to give himself reviews, the style of which he had read in American papers.

He would normally tell himself: "Superb with the power of genius... iridescent magnificence, defining the very role itself." The role Chiun was defining at this moment was that of the wounded flower in his 3,008-page poem that had already been rejected by twenty-two American publishers. An insensitive bee had plucked his pollen too rapidly.

The poem was in old Korean, the Korean dialect uninfluenced by Japanese. Remo peered into the cabin and saw the crimson-and-gold kimono of Chiun's poetry robe. He saw the long fingernails gracefully glide into the positions of a flower and then the flutter of a bee. He saw the wisps of white hair and the faint long delicate beard and realized that the deadliest assassin in the world had a visitor.

He looked farther around through the little porthole and he saw the shined black cordovan shoes on the carpet. The visitor was Dr. Harold W. Smith.

Remo let the director sit through another half hour of the Ung poetry, which Smith could not possibly understand because he did not know Korean. But such was Smith's great ability to deal with government figures that he could sit appearing interested hours on end, listening to what had to be to him just discordant sounds. He could have been hearing a record of dishes being washed and gotten as much real information from it. But here he was, eyebrows curled, thin lips pursed, head cocked ever so slightly, as if he were taking notes at a college lecture.

At a pause, Remo entered amid Smith's applause.

"Did you get the significance of that, Smitty?" asked Remo.

"I'm not familiar with the form," said Smith, "but what I do understand, I appreciate."

"What do you understand?" Remo asked.

"The hand movements. They were a flower, I assume," said Smith.

Chiun nodded. "Yes. Some are uncultured dregs and others have sensitivity. Perhaps it is my special burden that I am condemned to teach those who least appreciate it. That I, to earn tribute for my village as my ancestors before me, must squander the wisdom of Sinanju before the ingrate who has just arrived. Diamonds in the mud. A pale piece of a pig's ear, here before you."

"*Barf*," said Remo, in the manner of the Americans.

"Ah, you see, here the gratitude," said Chiun to Smith with a satisfied nod.

Smith leaned forward. His lemony face was even more somber than usual.

"I imagine you are wondering why I would appear here before both of you, so close to a spot where I assume you have just completed an assignment. I have never done this before, as you both know. We go to great pains to keep ourselves and our operations from public knowledge. Public knowledge of our operations would ruin us. It would be an admission that our government operates illegally."

"Oh, Emperor Smith," said Chiun. "He who holds the strongest sword makes his slightest whim legal."

Smith nodded in respect. This always amused Remo, when Smith tried to explain democracy to Chiun. For the House of Sinanju had served only kings and despots, the only ones with enough money to pay tribute to the assassins of Sinanju for the support of the village on rocky Korean coast. It did not occur to Remo at that moment that Smith was about to try to buy Chiun away from Remo, with fortunes far beyond those of petty kings and pharaohs.

"So I must be aboveboard in this," said Smith. "I have found you more and more difficult to deal with, Remo. Incredibly difficult."

Chiun smiled and his lined, aged face moved up and down in a nod. He noted that lo these many years he had endured Remo's lack of respect in gentle silence, not letting the world know what it was to give the great treasure of the knowledge of Sinanju to one who was so unworthy. Chiun compared himself, in his high squeaky voice, to the beautiful flower that his poem was about, how it was stepped on, to spring back uncomplaining with its beauty for the entire world.

"Good," said Smith. "I'd hoped you'd feel that way. I really did."

"I really don't give a ding dong," Remo said.

"In front of Emperor Smith, you say those things to a Master of Sinanju?" said Chiun. Gloom shrouded the parchment face and the Master of Sinanju lowered himself to the floor of the cabin, a delicate head rising up from a mushroom of crimson-and-gold robe. Underneath that kimono, Remo knew the long fingernails were woven together and the legs were crossed.

"All right," said Smith. "Gracious Master of Sinanju, you have created a marvel in Remo. You, as I, find it difficult to deal with him. I am prepared to offer you now ten times the tribute we ship to your village, if you will train others."

Chiun nodded, and smiled the thin calm acceptance of a flat warm lake in summer, waiting for the night to chill. This was due the House of Sinanju, Chiun said. And more was due.

"I will increase the tribute. Twenty times what we now pay," Smith said.

"Let me tell you something, Little Father," Remo said to Chiun. "The cost of the American submarine that delivers the gold to your village is more than the gold itself. He's not giving you that much."

"Fifty times the tribute," Smith said.

"See. See my worth," Chiun said to Remo. "What are you paid, white thing? Even your own whites offer me tribute tenfold. Twentyfold. A hundredfold. And you? Who offers you anything?"

"All right," said Smith who thought his last offer had been a fifty-times increase. "A hundredfold increase of eighteen-karat gold. That sort of gold is…"

"He knows, he knows," said Remo. "Give him a diamond and he can tell a flaw by holding it. He's a frigging jewelry store. He knows half the big stones in the world by heart. Telling Chiun about gold is like explaining the mass to the Pope."

"To support my poor village, I have become familiar to a degree with the value of things," Chiun said modestly.

"Ask him what a blue-white diamond, two karat flawless, sells for in Antwerp," said Remo to Smith. "Go ahead. Ask him."

"On behalf of the organization and the American people it serves, we are grateful to you, Chiun, Master of Sinanju. And you, Remo, you will receive a large stipend every year for the rest of your life. You will remain in retirement. You may die in bed of old age, knowing you have served your country well."

"I don't believe you," said Remo. "I believe I'll get the first check and maybe the second and then one day I'll open the door and the steps will blow up in my face. That's what I believe."

Remo loomed over Smith and let his left hand float under Smith's chin so Smith would realize Remo was willing to kill with that hand right now. He wanted his body presence to dominate Smith. But the stern man was not about to be dominated by a threat. His voice did not waver as he repeated the offer to the man who had taken the organization so far by himself. In Remo, the organization had the ultimate killer arm, the human being maximized to its highest potential. How Chiun had gotten this from Remo, Smith did not know. But if he could do it with one, he could do it with others.

"I'll tell you what I'm offering, Smitty," Remo said. "I'm leaving. And if you don't try to kill me, I won't kill you. But if by chance someone within five feet of me is poisoned or a taxi runs out of control on a street that I'm walking on or if a random shot is fired somewhere near me during a holdup, I am going to tell the world about an organization called CURE, that tried to make government work outside the Constitution. And how nothing got better and everything got worse, except a few bodies here and there got lost. Somewhere. I don't know where. And then I'm going to squeeze your lemon lips into your lemon heart and we'll be even. So goodbye."

"I'm sorry you feel that way, Remo. I've known you felt that way for some time. When did it all start? If you don't mind my asking."

"When people couldn't walk the frigging streets and I'm running around after some secret somewhere. The country isn't working. A man puts in forty hours a week to hear some son of a bitch tell him he's got no right to eat meat, but he's got to take the food off his table and give it to people who hang around all day and call him names. Enough. And that son of a bitch who tells him that, chances are, is on some public payroll somewhere making a thousand dollars a week saying how rotten this country is. No more."

"All right," said Smith sadly. "Thank you for what you have done."

"You're welcome," said Remo, without any kind feeling in it. He removed himself from over Smith and when he looked back he saw perspiration glint in the noonday sun off Smith's pale brow. Good, Remo thought. Smith had tasted fear. He had just been too proud to show it.

"And now for you, Master of Sinanju," Smith said.

Chiun nodded and spoke: "We accept your gracious offer but we have unfortunately fallen into an economic peculiarity and this distresses us so much. While we would be most happy to train hundreds, thousands, we cannot afford to. We have put more than a decade of work into this," said Chiun, nodding to Remo, "and we must protect that investment, worthless as it may seem to anyone."

"Five hundred times what your village gets now," Smith said. "And that probably means two submarines to deliver it."

"You can make it a million times more," said Remo. "He's not going to train your men. He might waltz a few people around, but he's not giving them Sinanju."

"Correct," said Chiun, elated. "I will never teach another white man Sinanju because of the disgusting ingratitude of this one. Therefore, no. I will stay with this ingrate."

"But you can be free of him and richer," Smith said. "I know of the House of Sinanju. You have done business for centuries."

"Centuries upon centuries," corrected Chiun.

"And this is more money," Smith said.

"He's not leaving me," said Remo. "I'm the best he's ever had. Better than Koreans he's had. If he could have found a decent Korean to take his place someday, he never would have gone to work for you."

"Is that true?" Smith asked.

"Nothing a white man says is true, except of course your gloriousness, oh Emperor."

"It's true," Remo said. "Besides, he's not leaving me. He likes me."

"Hah," said Chiun imperiously. "I stay to protect my investment in that unworthy white skin. That is why the Master of Sinanju stays."

Smith stared at his briefcase. Remo had never seen the human computer so thoughtful. Finally he looked up with a small tight-lipped smile.

"I guess we're stuck with each other, Remo," he said.

"Maybe," said Remo.

"You're the only one who can do what's got to be done," Smith said.

"I'll listen but I'm not promising," Remo said.

"It's all sort of sticky. We're not sure what we're looking for."

"So what else is new?" Remo asked.

Smith nodded glumly. "About a week ago, an old lady living in a poor neighborhood was tortured to death. It happened in the Bronx, and now agents from many nations were looking for an object or device that old woman must have had. The device had been brought to this country by her husband, a German refugee, who had died shortly before she did."

The sun lowered red over the Pacific ocean and still Smith talked. When he stopped, the stars were out.

And Remo said he would do the job, if he felt like it in the morning.

Smith nodded again, as he rose to his feet.

"Goodbye, Remo. Good luck," he said.

"Luck. You don't understand luck," Remo said contemptuously.

"And America bids respect and honor to the awesome magnificence of the Master of Sinanju," Smith said to Chiun.

"Of course," said Chiun.

ABOUT THE AUTHORS

WARREN MURPHY (1933 – 2015) was born in Jersey City, where he worked in journalism and politics until launching the **Destroyer** series with Richard Sapir in 1971. A screenwriter (*Lethal Weapon II*, *The Eiger Sanction*) as well as a novelist, Murphy's work won a dozen national awards, including multiple Edgars and Shamuses. He was a lecturer at many colleges and universities; his lessons on writing a novel are available on his website, WarrenMurphy.com. A Korean War veteran, some of Murphy's many hobbies included golf, mathematics, opera, and investing. He served on the board of the Mystery Writers of America, and was a member of the Screenwriters Guild, the Private Eye Writers of America, the International Association of Crime Writers, and the American Crime Writers League. He has five children: Deirdre, Megan, Brian, Ardath, and Devin.

RICHARD BEN SAPIR was a New York native who worked as an editor and in public relations, before creating *The Destroyer* series with Warren Murphy. Before his untimely death in 1987, Sapir had also penned a number of thriller and historical mainstream novels, best known of which were *The Far Arena*, *Quest* and *The Body*, the last of which was made recently into a film. The New York Times book review section called him "a brilliant professional."

Made in the USA
Coppell, TX
01 March 2023

13541855R00085